D1519947

Help us Rate this book...
Put your initials on the
left side and your rating
on the right side.
  1 = Didn't care for
  2 = It was O.K.
  3 = It was <u>great</u>

E TEMPEST PASSES

E WICKED IS NO MORE

_____ℓ___   1 2 ③
____am___   1 2 ③
_____   1 2 3
_____   1 2 3
_____   1 2 3
_____   1 2 3
_____   1 2 3
_____   1 2 3
_____   1 2 3
_____   1 2 3
_____   1 2 3   PHART-NASH
_____   1 2 3
_____   1 2 3
_____   1 2 3
_____   1 2 3

Outskirts Press, Inc.
http://www.outskirtspress.com

Paperback ISBN: 978-1-9772-3488-9
Hardback ISBN: 978-1-9772-3420-9

Outskirts Press and the "OP" logo are trademarks belonging to Outskirts Press, Inc.

New roman-`a-clef true novel based on the life of Olena Hogenson Erickson through memories and imagination of her granddaughter. A family's unsolved mystery. Families are complex, puzzling, mysterious, sometimes admired, and sometimes disliked. Some memories are recalled with love and gratitude, others with feelings of fear and sometimes dislike. Always there was something hinted at, sometimes whispered about, not quite talked about. Mysterious--but definitely there. Her grandmother is central, a silent figure full of sadness and loss, but beneath the surface was a world of other unresolved emotions. This story is shared with the hope that she attained peace at the end of her life as writing about it has brought peace of mind to the granddaughter.

*I would like to dedicate this book to
my grandmother and all silenced women.*

FOREWORD

It is with deep gratefulness and endless thanks to Curt Swarm, Danette Hennigar, and Johanna Denning I give the credit for the completion of this book. It has lived in my head for 60 years, disrupting my sleep to the point of hearing myself wearily say one pre-dawn, "Who are you people and what do you want?" That was when I took my daughter, Danni's (Danette) advice and signed up for a creative writing class offered by Curt Swarm: Author, Columnist, Metal Sculptor, Photographer. Thank you, Curt, for helping me find the courage to put my thoughts and memories on paper. For seven weeks I hardly left my basement—writing into the wee hours of the morning. Then watched my husband reading everything I dumped on my kitchen counter the next day, I am so grateful for his wonderful encouragement. I am sorry for all the days I consumed of my generous daughter's life as she put everything in order and into the computer after Curt edited the whole story. Add 'Editor' to Curt's accomplishments. Thank you so much, Curt.

And last but certainly not least, I thank my wonderfully talented granddaughter, Johanna Denning, for her evocative design for the book cover. As busy as she is with her own life and business, "Gush Creative," she took on one more job for Grandma! Thank you, Jo.

I owe you all a debt of gratitude.

Mange-takk!

TABLE OF CONTENTS

Ecclesiastes 3:1
"For everything there is a season, and a time for
every matter under heaven..."

FAMILY TREE OF CHARACTERS

1. Ole Hogenson (1888-1911)
m. ˜1874 Karen "Carrie" Olson (1846-1908)
  ⊢2. Hannah Bertine Hogenson (1876-1881)
  ⊢2. Olena "Lena" Matilda Hogenson (1877-1956)
    m. 1900 Cornelius H Erickson (1863-1949)
    ⊢3. Henry Orlando Erickson (1901-1909)
    ⊢3. Clarence Bernhardt Erickson (1903-1904)
    ⊢3. Clarence Bernhard Erickson (1905-1958)
     m.Vera L Snure
    ⊢3. Lloyd Cornelius Erickson (1908-1970)
    ⊢3. Helen Gladys Erickson (1911-1997)
     m. 1984 Clarence Raymond "Ray" Kephart (1912-
      ⊢4. Jason Kephart (1935-1984)
      ⊢4. Linda Kephart (1937-)
      ⊢4. Karen Kephart (1940-)
    ⊢3. Olga Christina Erickson (1917-1988)
     m.Jacob "Jake" Isaac Kephart (1915-1978)
      ⊢4. Donald Kephart (1939-1977)
      ⌞4. Merrilee Kephart (1937-)
  ⊢2. Hendriek "Henry" Hogenson (1879-1897)
  ⌞2. Olga Christena Hogenson (1884-1910)

1. Hans Eriksen (1888-1911)
m. ˜1860 Maren (1834-1925)
  ⊢2. Ingeborg Isabelle "Belle" Erickson (1860-1940)
  ⊢2. Cornelius H Erickson (1863-1949)
    m. 1900 Olena "Lena" Matilda Hogenson (1877-
    ⊢3. Henry Orlando Erickson (1901-1909)
    ⊢3. Clarence Bernhardt Erickson (1903-1904)
    ⊢3. Clarence Bernhard Erickson (1905-1958)
     m.Vera L Snure
    ⊢3. Lloyd Cornelius Erickson (1908-1970)
    ⊢3. Helen Gladys Kephart Erickson (1911-1997)
     m. 1984 Clarence Raymond "Ray" Kephart
      ⊢4. Jason Kephart (1935-1984)
      ⊢4. Linda Kephart (1937-)
      ⊢4. Karen Kephart (1940-)
    ⌞3. Olga Christina Erickson (1917-1988)
     m.Jacob "Jake" Isaac Kephart (1915-1978)
      ⊢4. Donald "Donnie" Kephart (1939-1977)
      ⌞4. Merrilee Kephart (1937-)
  ⊢2. Emma Martine Erickson (1867-?)
    m. Birt Newman
  ⊢2. Erick Erickson (1872-1919)
    m. Caroline Erickson (?-?)
  ⊢2. Karen Clara Erickson "Carrie" (1875-1953)
    m. Christian "Chris" Bidsler (1864-1945)
    ⊢3. Hildus Bidsler (1904-1986)
    ⌞3. "Bernie" Bidsler (˜1910-1916)
  ⌞2. Herman Martinius Eriksen (1875-1972)
    m. Hilda M Erickson (˜1878-1940)

Karen Hogenson with Lena and Olga

Maren and Hans Erickson

INTRODUCTION

*W*here to begin? How? I am older now than she was when she died. My maternal grandmother, Olena Matilda Hogenson Erickson. And yes, she was Norwegian. There has not been a time in my long life that I have not thought about her, wondered how she endured. What must she have felt in the bitterness and betrayal of someone she deeply loved? And of the rage and hate that became her daily existence in a loveless marriage.

It's possible I have misjudged those in my memory that pass by in the company of my grandmother. I was only a child at the time, but I had eyes and ears; a vivid memory of all things; and I suspect I was also an invasive nuisance from the number of times some relative would remark on my entrance to a room about there being "Many ears in a cornfield!" I will begin at the end.

1956

A TIME TO BE BORN
AND A TIME TO DIE

*A*nd that is in a very small hospital in a small town in Rushford, Minnesota--August 22nd, 1956. She was dying, a 78-year-old woman whose body had become a burden too much. Her bones leached of calcium, crumbled, collapsed... shrinking a tall, graceful girl to a bent, crooked-backed woman with uneven, painful steps. A broken hip had brought her to the hospital, and now in delirium--awkwardly propped in the bed because of the deformed back and accommodation for the broken hip--medicated as much as possible against the pain. The family waited. Both her daughters, Helen and Olga, sat by her bed, sometimes alone, sometimes together. And both the sons, Clarence and Lloyd, watching silently, grieving inwardly. She was a mother greatly loved by her four surviving children. Her children had been her one singular love and joy in a long and unhappy marriage; they seemed to form a silent shield around her over the years. And I wondered about that, as at times I didn't like her; sometimes I did--but mostly I felt invisible to her. But she was not thus to me.

I do not know which of those three days of waiting that the singing of the lullabies occurred, but her daughter,

Helen--my mother, told me of her lovely singing voice. How in her delirium, with a clear, strong voice she began to sing the beautiful lullabies she had sung in Norwegian for all her babies so many years ago. And, how the songs drew the nurses, and strangers, to the doorway of the dying woman. The body a wreckage, the voice still so beautiful.

Helen wept often, unable to keep from it as she blamed herself for the accident. Olga scolded, saying, "For God's sake, Helen! You were sick, you needed sleep!"

And Helen did look sick with red nose, bleary eyes, and a fever blister. Another bad head cold; it seemed she caught every cold that made the rounds. But this time, having helped her mother down for an afternoon nap, had herself fallen asleep on the sofa just outside her mother's bedroom door and not heard her call later for help to get up. And so--the fall from the bed had happened, and the hip fracture.

In three days the funeral was underway. The ancient undertaker in response to the family's gratitude for his excellent skill said, "I remember how beautiful she was.

"And I remember the fine bones of her face, the slender, delicate nose, intelligent brow, and very blue eyes. I remember thin gray hair in a braided bun, but heard her hair was pale golden to her waist at one time.

And so, she was buried in the Highland Prairie Lutheran Cemetery in Minnesota--where all her former family now lies: her parents, Ole and Karen, five-year-old Hannah whose dying request had been for a headstone on her grave; Hendriek, her handsome, protective brother, drowned at age 18. And beloved sister, Olga--laughing, impetuous--gone at 21.

But Olena's husband is buried miles away, in his family cemetery in Hesper, Iowa. It is where my own parents, Ray and Helen are, also my brother, Jason.

Highland Prairie, MN I have visited several times, and always come away sad and downcast. I believe most likely over little Hannah who never got her headstone. Near a wire fence, in the shade of a nearby tree, my mother pointed out an area said to be where the small body is. Her death from consumption came some short while after Ole and Karen, farmers, emigrated from Norway to Choice in Minnesota; a particularly good area to grow wheat, which our government under then President Hayes--or perhaps Grant-- wanted and promoted, and to which Norwegian farmers responded to such a degree that the southeastern corner of Minnesota and northeastern corner of Iowa were jokingly called "Little Norway".

But times were hard during this period of history and for a long time money was hard to come by. Simply put, there was no money for a little girl's last request, so she lies in an unmarked grave. And that still grieves me. I've wondered if the Angel headstone I saw on an old grave there was one Hannah saw, and later hoped one like it would mark her resting place. There are two other graves in that cemetery that shattered Olena's heart so many years ago. Henry, eight, was Olena's first son, and Clarence Bernhard, one-and-a-half-year-old, was her second-born. Mothers never get over losing a child. And a third grave is missing altogether. But not forgotten. And now I'll go into the distant past.

1895

A TIME TO PLANT AND A TIME TO PLUCK UP

He kept his thoughts to himself, tamping down any frustration over circumstances he had no control over as he doggedly pursued the course he'd set for himself. He hated being poor, always working another man's land; hated the feeling of being looked down on. Today he had time to mull over in his mind how to approach in a favorable way a Mr. Hogenson. He very much wanted the hired hand position he'd heard the farmer outside Choice was looking to fill. Jolting along on the hard seat of his buggy with the steady clip-clop of the horse's hooves in his ears, he had plenty of time to do a lot of thinking. He had worked so hard since arriving in Winneshiek County, Iowa when he was 16, such a long way from Norway. He'd had to learn English, struggle in school, help his father on their patch of land to grow the wheat they had all come to America to grow. He was oldest of three sons, but Erik and Herman did not want the labor-intensive life of their father and had left as soon as they could.

He felt sorry for Belle, three years older than himself. Ingeborg Isabelle--how she hated that name! So she was just "Belle". Odd, didn't seem to fit. Any hope for marriage was left behind in Norway when she came to Iowa at the age of 19. A blessing for their mother, though, as Maren's eyesight slowly faded, and she needed her daughter's help more each passing day. If Belle's lot in life distressed her, she kept that to herself; but she gave of her time and energy generously; a kind and gentle woman who left everyone who'd been in her company feeling happier and somehow better about things. Belle. She was his favorite sibling. Their mother had often related how Belle had claimed Cornelius as her own baby from the time she was three and got her first look at him. Always his protector and guide as a toddler. He, himself, had chosen the single life; focusing on working and saving. AND having his own land someday. There wasn't time or money for wife or family.

When he thought of Erik, he felt the acid of jealousy. Erik at 24 had sought his fortune in Minot, North Dakota with some success, having no interest in the hard life of a farmer; and he very much enjoyed dressing in fine suits and stiff white-collared shirts, and always a really fine hat on his head. He looked quite the dandy. And showing off his success, he lured Herman into following him to Minot. Cornelius felt pride in his brother, but also recognized the envy he felt at the extreme differences in their circumstances. Recently, Emma had married and was now out of the homestead, but Carrie was still there and as eager to get on with life as their brothers had been. He was glad Emma had married a good man, very decent. Everyone had whole-heartedly welcomed Birt into the family.

Things were changing and he too wanted change. He had been saving for sixteen years and had looked at many parcels of land scattered around parts of Iowa and Minnesota. One piece looked promising on the west side of Mabel in Minnesota. Terrible access though. Almost straight up the steep hill to the large Victorian house perched like a beacon at the very top. On the east side it could only be pasture it was so steep. Poking up from deep in the earth at the pinnacle of the hill was a gigantic, pitted rock many feet high. A mystery as the land all about was not rocky. But all the acres north of the house and hill was gently rolling hills--perfect for wheat or corn. It had a good barn, hen house, corncrib, pigpen, windmill, and apple orchard. Yes. A very nice place; and the owners were an elderly couple with one son, who was having health issues. He hoped the bank would look favorably on the loan he knew he would be asking for. No point dwelling further on that.

He hoped Hogenson would be readily available. But he could as well be out in a field. Or in town. He might be in for a wait to see the man. He'd dressed in his one good church suit, and his only white shirt. A borrowed hat was tucked safely down by his feet. He hoped he wouldn't be covered in dust by the time he got to the Hogenson farm. And he also hoped he wouldn't have to look for nighttime lodging. He worked too hard to waste money. A jug of water and home baked bread with cheese lay wrapped in a white cloth in a box behind his seat.

When the sun was directly overhead, he'd guided the horse into a farmyard to a horse tank and called to a woman busy at her clothesline if his horse could have water and a short rest in the shade. She nodded, and continued with her work while he sat in the buggy eating his lunch, tipping the quart jar of water to his mouth periodically, pausing to wipe the crumbs and moisture away with a clean white handkerchief from a large mustache covering his entire upper lip.

The trip was nearing its end, finally. He'd seen a sign bearing the name "Choice" and knew he was nearing the town as more homes and gardens came into sight. He hoped to see someone who could point him in the right direction to the Hogenson farmstead, but was beginning to think he'd be in town limits before anyone would appear. However, when cresting a low hill he spotted someone working in a garden next to a small run-down house. He'd passed a few like it, mixed with others kept neat and painted. Now he turned the horse's head towards the dirt track leading to the house, and to a worn-looking woman in a weedy garden. A ragamuffin girl with matted hair stood silently as her mother straightened and turned hard eyes on the stranger in her yard. He was polite in asking for the information he needed, and the woman did indeed know the farm and gave him the needed directions. Carefully backing and turning the buggy--with the young girl following, and staring--Cornelius became aware of an urchin of a boy sitting on the low roof of the house, watching everything. The absurdity of it stopped him and, puzzled, he asked the girl why the boy--no doubt her brother--was on the roof? And taking much time to answer--he was about to continue out the dirt track with no explanation--when she said, "'Cause he gets a beatin' when he comes down." To which Cornelius had to ask, "And what did he do to deserve the beating?" But apparently, she was through talking as she shrugged her thin shoulders indifferently and with no expression on her face returned to her mother. He looked again at the silent lump sitting on the roof, glanced at the care-worn figure who'd returned to her battle with nature in the garden, then "clicked" at the horse, gave a flick of the rein and left the dreary scene behind. "Spare the rod and spoil the child" was an echo in his head. He'd taken a few beatings of his own, and survived. Plus a couple not his own. He'd been raised in the Lutheran Church, was a faithful attender, and was in his third year as trustee. It had been fairly recent that he'd heard a sermon on the "spare-the-rod" theme, and the thought came that maybe he'd been "spared-a-lot" by not marrying and having to civilize a brood of children. Boys in particular. They seemed to be the most troublesome.

Following the woman's directions he turned back the direction he'd come. He'd passed the farm's turn-off about a mile back. Well, it could have been worse--could have been further--could be pouring rain. Best not to be complaining.

With sharp eyes he took in the straight fences around well-tended fields, and grazing land. Turning into the wide dirt road to a white two-story farmhouse set apart from a near red barn, with outbuildings not far apart, he recognized that Mr. Hogenson was a good farmer, diligent in his care of the land and buildings. He hoped the job hadn't been taken yet, and he also hoped room and board was included. That would greatly help towards the farm he so desired for himself.

Leaving horse and buggy in the shade of a tree near the house, Cornelius, with borrowed hat set firmly on his head, walked a neat stone path leading to the side of the house, apparently to the kitchen, and stepping up several stairs, stood at the back door. As he raised a hand to knock, he saw a figure approaching the door, shadowy behind the screen, and lowered his hand. He introduced himself to the unseen person and explained his mission whereupon Mrs. Karen Hogenson introduced herself and invited him in, saying her husband was not far away and one of the children would be sent for him.

Cornelius thought her a very pleasant woman, and efficiency seemed part of her nature for she had immediately called out to a daughter somewhere in the house saying, "Olga, go now for Papa. There is a man here to see him. Oh! And tell Hendriek to water Mr. Erickson's horse! Hurry now!" He heard quick footsteps clatter down stairs somewhere in the house; and into the kitchen came a rush of energy topped with a mop of wild auburn curls, wide brown eyes, and a swish of skirts. He thought her age to be about ten or twelve. Later he learned he was right: she was 11. And Olga, he later found out, had enough energy and curiosity to keep things stirred to a simmer most of the times and worse, some of the time. Now the screen door slammed behind her, and on turning his head he could see her at a dead run, skirts flying, headed for the barn.

Chatting with Mrs. Hogenson was pleasant, and Cornelius found himself enjoying the relaxing minutes talking with this interesting woman. He found it easy asking questions of the area, the small town of Choice; and also of Norway, something in common for them both. When Olga returned it was to say that "Pa" wanted Mr. Erikson to meet with him in the barn, so the friendly visit with the lady of the house was over, and Olga assigned herself the office of escorting Cornelius to her father. He strongly suspected the girl's curiosity and needing to hear everything was what motivated her eager assistance. And it wasn't long before he was proved right, as her father, in a kind way, but firm, directed her back to the house. She dragged her feet, not happy.

Mr. Hogenson extended a hand to Cornelius, all the while studying the muscled man standing before him. He looked decent enough, and strong. Obviously clean, neat, and had taken pains to be presentable. If there was one thing Cornelius had learned from Erik, it was that appearance very much matters. Questions went back and forth; and soon both men were on first name basis.

Ole believed a man's handshake was as good as his word. And this man had looked him in the eye as he gave a firm grip in return. He liked what he heard, glad for the similar backgrounds, and especially relieved to know the man was not a drinker and was a Godly church-going Lutheran, as was his own family. A tour of the neat farm followed with explanation of all that would be expected of him should he accept the job. Pay was discussed and found acceptable to Cornelius. He had been relieved to know there was a small bunkroom to the front east corner of the barn. It was clean, had a small window, a door with a lock, bed, and wall pegs for clothes, a shelf, one chair, and a washstand. The only drawback was lack of heat in winter, he would need to take a room in Choice but, at least most of the time, here is where he could lodge free. And meals would be with the Hogensons. Ole gave him the names of two elderly spinster sisters who rented their spare rooms to make ends meet. And so it was, Cornelius was embarking on a change in his own life. No more living with parents. It felt right; and he felt as though some sort of weight--he hadn't even been aware of--lifted from his shoulders. Ole, too, was pleased, feeling he had been lucky to find a hired hand he liked.

Ready to begin the return trip, Cornelius found his horse had been cared for--fed and watered by a slender boy with light brown hair that Ole introduced as Hendriek, his son. He seemed shy, or maybe he was simply quiet by nature. He didn't talk much, but had a disquieting way of studying the stranger, showing neither a liking nor a disliking of Cornelius. He certainly wasn't a whirlwind of energy like his little sister. Another daughter, Olena, was away and he had yet to meet her.

The return journey was in a more relaxed feeling, and plans were running through his mind on the changes he would need to attend to. He would have to resign his trustee position in the church. His term was nearly up anyway.

Methodical and already pretty much set in his ways, he made the necessary preparations for moving to his new living arrangements--feeling quite content actually. He had so very few possessions. There had been no need to accrue unneeded baggage. As to clothing, he had all that was needed. He owned his horse and buggy, the worn trunk containing the clothing. And the old wooden "sailor's desk" he'd come into possession of on the ship bringing him when he was sixteen, along with his family from Vinderen, Vestre Aker in Norway. Painted Nordic blue and dull red with the old sailor's initials and date on it. The old fellow had simply gone to sleep one night and didn't wake up. What few possessions he'd had were offered to whoever wanted them. He now lay in a watery grave, forgotten. The desk had a small brass key and lock. The key Cornelius kept on a leather fob attached to a cheap pocket watch. In it were all that he deemed important: citizenship papers, receipts for horse and buggy, address book of family members, bible--and his one vice, a pipe and pouch of tobacco. He felt entitled to this harmless indulgence which he'd picked up while socializing with other men at the voting stations.

He never missed voting for each new American president. He considered himself neither Democrat nor Republican. He hadn't voted for Grover Cleveland, a Democrat, but the man seemed to be doing a good job. Tough on corruption--and God knew that was a BIG problem. And he certainly wasn't fearful of using the power of his veto like a hammer. No, Cleveland was a good President.

The trustee position had been dealt with, and he felt gratified by the many "thank yous," handshakes, well wishes and good-byes at Sunday's service. His sister and mother had been quite emotional, while his father had simply reached out and squeezed his shoulder. Now he was well on his way, and as the horse trotted steadily north-northwest, Cornelius pulled out the pipe and carefully tamped tobacco into its bowl. Then cupping his hand and twisting his torso to shield it from the breeze he lit it on the second wooden match.

It was late afternoon when he pulled the buggy in by the Hogenson barn, and was surprised by Hendriek's appearance. He'd come to help Cornelius settle into the bunk house, and to see to the horse and buggy. Ole must have arranged for the boy to meet him and make sure all went well. The quiet watchfulness of the boy made Cornelius uneasy, but surely in time they would become accustomed to one another's ways and the awkwardness would pass.

Now Hendriek spoke, "Supper at 6:00. Water to wash up is at the pump house." With his message delivered he disappeared.

Taking out the watch, Cornelius knew he could put up his clothes and at least have that done. With the metal trunk set at the foot of the bed and the wooden desk box with slanted lid stowed on the shelf under the washstand, he put his shaving mug with its round lathering brush, the straight razor leather strop, comb, brush and mirror in the single drawer of the wash stand, and looked around the room. Someone had placed clean towels that hung from the bars on each side of the stand, and the bed was made up with an extra folded blanket at the foot. And on the pillow was a key for the door which he picked up and slipped into a pocket. He debated with himself about locking the door and decided he would do so only at night. Or...no, perhaps it was best to keep the door locked whenever he was out as he remembered the impulsive, curious Olga. The two Hogenson children he'd met were of such extremely different temperaments it caused him to wonder what the third one was like. A teenage girl. That much he knew.

The washing up had been in cold water, but better than nothing. Now he approached the screen door to the kitchen, but it popped open before he reached it and to no surprise, Olga welcomed him in to the table now set for six. The aroma of fried chicken, and fresh bread was wonderful, and it mingled with other tantalizing smells making him suddenly hungry. Karen greeted him cheerfully saying, "Ole will be right down."

Hendriek stood, waiting, at his chair and that was the moment Cornelius' chosen well-planned path for his life splintered into two paths, leaving him suspended in time, disoriented and momentarily speechless. Carrying the platter of chicken was the most beautiful girl Cornelius had ever seen. Tall. Taller than he was, willowy, graceful, with a porcelain doll face and blue eyes and pale golden hair almost to her waist. It was all tied back with a ribbon that matched her eyes.

He tried to recall her name as he struggled to think of something to say. Behind him he heard Ole greet him, and, dazed, he turned to answer, and didn't miss the odd gaze from Hendriek. At least Ole was unaware of the effect the girl had had on him, as was Karen. And Olga had been busy pulling her chair to the table. Olena. That was the name. And Olena hadn't caught his stare either. But Hendriek had!

Now he was under control again and entered into the easy camaraderie of this close family. Olena smiled and dipped her head in a little nod at the introduction, and then resumed eating. But from that moment, Cornelius' head was filled with thoughts of Olena. For the love of God, he was 33. He now knew she was 17.

And so Cornelius settled into a new life, a new routine. And he kept his thoughts to himself. At all times he was careful not to look too much at the girl and never went out of his way to be near her. He knew to break those rules would be his fastest way off the farm and out of a job that he was determined not to leave. He went out of his way to charm Karen; made himself indispensable to Ole; teased and entertained Olga. But Hendriek distanced himself and remained aloof. It became clear to Cornelius that Hendriek was conveniently present whenever Olena happened into Cornelius' company. It was obvious Hendriek did not like Cornelius.

It was pleasant adjusting to the new life with the Hogensons. One could not have met nicer people. And attending church with them at Highland Prairie Lutheran was where he would have been even without them. He did choose to take his own horse and buggy so as not to crowd them and risk becoming burdensome. Cornelius was comfortable in the small church that thrived in the rural countryside, with farmland on all sides in the gently rolling hills. A white wooden church with belfry and steeple was built on land donated by a devout landowner. Every Sunday morning the sound of the bell carried over the hills and valleys, calling the faithful to service, and come they did, filling the pews, wearing their best. Tall pines formed a wind break on the north side. A variety of deciduous trees were scattered around the cemetery behind the church. Already there were many headstones. Most very small, a few larger, and one that drew the eyes toward it. An almost life-size statue of an angel with wings folded, eyes gazing down. Such a peaceful setting.

Olga had led Cornelius there to admire the angel--apparently drawn to it herself. And chattering as only she could, she told him of Hannah, the sister she never met, who had died of consumption at the age of five. Then pointing a finger towards the side of the cemetery, all the while beckoning him to follow, stopped by a slightly sunken area near a young tree by the fence. There she told him Hannah had asked for and been promised a headstone for her grave.

He had asked then why this had not been done since it was promised.

Thinking about the question for a moment Olga answered, "No money then. Besides, she is with Jesus now and that's all that matters."

And then Hendriek was there, a strange fire in his eyes. Tight-lipped he told Olga she was being waited on for the return home.

Cornelius watched their retreating backs, then looked down at the small sunken area, and couldn't help thinking, "A promise made should be a promise kept." But then again, as Olga said--what did it matter now?

Cornelius had joined the Highland Prairie Lutheran Church and almost instantly been recruited as usher. Always cognizant of fitting in and being accepted, he'd taken on the role of ushering; and felt well received by other members. One other thing he was aware of always was Olena. It was never easy, but he avoided looking directly at her, and never sought her company. To all appearances he was just a polite, respectable Christian man attending worship faithfully in the company of his employer and family, all of whom appeared fond of him. He had proved to be an ideal hired hand any employer would have been grateful to have. The work was hard, and the weather could be difficult some days but Ole was a good man to work for, and the farm itself a delight and wisely managed. A large, swift creek ran through a portion of the land, too deep to ride a horse through, so a railless wood bridge had been laid across the noisy stream for easy access to the property on the other side. It was also a shortcut into Choice by horseback. Cornelius had become familiar with all the land; and dreamed all the more of when he had land of his own.

Mealtime was more difficult. Especially with the quiet

Hendriek whose eyes missed nothing. The ever-bubbly Olga always kept the conversation moving with observations and opinions about everything--which led to often-times being encouraged to "value silence," or a "Please, just finish your meal!" from her parents.

Olena's interests ran deeper. She brought books home from the nearest library, and of late had been puzzling over why women couldn't vote. She took that omission seriously. That was just wrong in her opinion!

Cornelius wondered how she perceived him; did she like him? He couldn't tell. Think him respectable? Trustworthy? The wondering was a form of torture.

Had he asked she would not have told him all her thoughts of him, out of kindness. Olena did view him as a man of good manners, obviously well brought up. He was indeed a man who practiced cleanliness, and was self-disciplined, which she admired--admired also that he lived an orderly Christian life. He seemed a decent man. But attractive to her he was not. She knew it was a sin to judge anyone by their outward appearance; and she felt some shame over thinking what a short man he was. Short. And thick. And she did not like hair on any male face, even knowing it was the fashion. His thick, wide, bushy, reddish mustache repelled her. Of course no one can help what color hair they are born with; that really is unimportant. Olga's hair was called auburn, full of curls and waves, and she thought her sister was quite lovely. Cornelius' hair was a close match to Olga's, also with deep waves and curls. His skin had become rough and sun-darkened from working in all manner of weather.

But it was his eyes that disturbed her; small, close-set, dark, and secretive. Always sliding away. No. he was not attractive to her in any way. And she did her best to keep her distance. Eyes were said to be the windows to the soul. Lately she had begun wondering if Hendriek had formed some manner of dislike towards Cornelius. It was just an odd feeling she had.

Olena did not like her names--none of them. She had complained to her mother, "It isn't bad enough to name me Lena--you had to call me O-lena Matilda! PAH!" She could get angry, and that was one of her peeves. But she did prefer the O to be left off.

Lena had begged for a piano and piano lessons; neither were forthcoming. In church though her beautiful singing voice did not go un-noticed and the choir director offered her music lessons if she would join the choir. And so she did; and made as frequent trips as she could to his home for lessons and practice. But it would be a while before a piano would arrive.

That first winter of '95-'96 Cornelius had the use of one of Ole's horses to come and go daily by the short cut over the wooden planks across the frozen stream. The echo of hooves on the wood as well as the visual alteration in crossing over the water was very much disturbing to any horse, so until it adjusted to it, it was led across the bridge. Over time several of Ole's horses came to accept it and could be ridden across.

The three Hogenson children made their way to and from school in a light rig and pony. But with Lena about to graduate, Hendriek had been working with a gentle mare to train her to cross the bridge for when he and Olga could ride double by the short cut. Hendriek had the patience to train the horse; and it had the disposition to be amenable, so the lessons were going very well.

Cornelius looked forward to being back in the bunk room--though the weeks of winter in a spare room of the two spinsters had gone well. He had no complaints; he would be glad to be back on the farm full-time. He had been open to Ole about his plan to eventually have his own farm, which had made a good impression on Ole. Spring work was under way, and farmers all around had repaired farm machinery, ordered seed, soon to be picked up. All were eager to be out in their fields.

While in the houses, wives waited for the days windows could be opened and fresh air blowing through the rooms. Rooms would be turned upside down for a good spring cleaning. Curtains would be taken down and washed, cobwebs brushed down, mattresses aired, rugs beaten on the clothesline.

With spring in the air lambs were bleating in the pastures. Near warm kitchen stoves, eggs about to hatch chicks were carefully rotated. There was something hopeful in the very air.

Cornelius reported to Karen that the spinster sister who had given piano lessons for many years was slipping in memory and would probably be selling the piano before much longer. Pausing in her work Karen thought this might be the time to think of a piano for Lena. And perhaps involving Olga in learning to play, too, might direct her into more genteel activities. Goodness knows the girl needed to be kept occupied. What a wild one! Karen couldn't stop the smile that spread across her face thinking, "But she is such fun--and so funny. How she loves to make people laugh." She would discuss the business of the piano with Ole later that night. Now she gathered up the fresh smelling laundry that she had folded and carried sheets and towels and undergarments up the stairs to be put away. As she passed the girl's bedroom, she heard the sweet sound of Lena singing one of Sunday's hymns. It seemed so easy for the girl to memorize songs. Karen gave a light tap and raised the door latch, entering her daughter's room, noting, almost in surprise, how grown up Lena was. Her 18th birthday had been about two weeks before: soon she would graduate from school. How fast the years had gone, and how well she and Ole had done. Putting down the sheets on the bed and other laundry on the dresser top, she wondered how serious Lena was about the nice-looking young man who made a point of talking to her after church the last two Sundays. Karen knew he came from a good background, attended church with his parents when he was home. And she'd heard no unpleasant gossip about him. Lena seemed shy around him. And being so fair, blushed much too easily which made Lena upset with herself. Karen suspected the attraction was mutual. Now she told her about the piano, asking if she was still interested in having one in the house. The delight in Lena's face was answer enough. On telling of her thoughts to maybe have lessons for Olga, Lena laughed saying, "No way will Olga go for that! But it wouldn't hurt to try anyway."

After the evening meal Cornelius made his way back to the barn; the sky was darkening and light would be needed in his room. A lantern, hung from the hook on a rafter, filled the small room with light. A small table had been added to his furnishings and was set against the wall. It held his collection of the newspapers he occasionally brought from town, and which he read, and read again. He missed nothing in them. And while he scoured the papers, he smoked. Bringing the pipe and tobacco pouch from out of the sailor's desk; tamping and lighting it in pleasant anticipation. There he sat by his table, sucking on the pipe stem, inhaling, exhaling, relaxing. And then his thoughts turned to Lena. He had perfected the art of concealing his obsession for the girl so that he hadn't a doubt in the world that anyone had guessed his secret. Except maybe--Hendriek. But as long as he said nothing--and apparently the boy did keep his mouth shut--no harm was done. But he hated those searching eyes!--taking his measure, it seemed. No amount of friendliness towards the boy changed anything in the slightest way. Best to leave sleeping dogs lie.

What had recently taken to bothering him more was what he noticed at church; and that was the attention to Lena from more than one dash-fire fool. He didn't like seeing them talk to her and hang around. Though it bothered less when he could see she was clearly disinterested.

But that changed with the appearance of the Henderson boy, home on break from college and attending church with his parents. He looked to be in his early twenties. Lena was different around him. Tall handsome Lars! An eye-catching couple--one so fair-haired, the other black-haired.

Cornelius' teeth clenched at the thought of Lars Henderson hanging around Lena. But he'd soon be going back to his college crowd. Cornelius could hardly wait for that day. He had his own plans and he was set upon them. Soon he readied for sleep and turned out the lantern.

1897

A TIME TO KILL AND
A TIME TO HEAL

Hendriek Hogenson, Brother of Lena

December had been set for the time Cornelius would visit his parents and celebrate the Christmas season with them. Maren was essentially blind, dependent on the patient sweet-natured Belle. If the weather cooperated his siblings would show up as well for a time of celebration, catching up, and feasting. He enjoyed the time with all of them but was restless with the need to be back in the midst of the Hogenson family, knowing a certain Lars Henderson was home for good, working for his father in their lumberyard-hardware store. And that he was calling frequently on Lena. And the knowing was unbearable. What he didn't know was they had been corresponding for over a year, and already marriage plans were underway.

The winter had been an especially harsh one. Getting out, to care for the animals, had been difficult for the men and during the time of the January blizzard Cornelius had been given a cot in the parlor for most of a week. It was an uncomfortable week under the watchfulness of Hendriek, but necessary for the feeding and milking of the many cows. As with all things the days slipped away, the weather eased up slowly, and the time passed pleasantly in the evenings with board games and caramelized popcorn.

March came in like a lamb, a welcome change in the hard Minnesota winter. Lena's 19th birthday was March 18th and she received birthday greetings from all her family, but no parties or gift-giving was done--nor was it expected. The secret she kept to herself hung on a fine ribbon around her neck, hidden under her clothes: an heirloom ring which had belonged to Lars' grandmother; a gift to her from her then-fiancé, its stone was a small emerald, Lars' grandmother's birthstone, set in gold. Lars' mother had asked if he wanted it for Lena. His feelings for Lena were well known in his family, all of whom teased him mercilessly. He had given her the ring in secret planning to first consult with Lena's father which was only respectful.

Cornelius had resumed his trips back to his room in town at night, and all things returned to usual. Olga had come down with a very bad cold with coughing and chills, missing church. Karen kept her home from school for several days, leaving Hendriek to ride the good-natured "Taffy" to school by himself.

Early the second morning he and "Taffy" departed the barn, and with a wave toward the kitchen window, disappeared down the lane. Night came, but Hendriek did not. Karen asked Ole if perhaps he was with Cornelius--it was a cold night after all; he may be staying there. But how unlike it was of him. Didn't he realize they would worry? Lena stated she doubted he would stay with Cornelius but didn't add any opinion as to why she would think that.

Too restless to begin his own bedtime preparations, Ole put on his heavy winter clothing, went out to the barn and saddled a horse. Then going by road to town, as this horse had never gone over the bridge--he left to look for his son. And an anxious mother waited.

Ole stopped at Cornelius' first and was told Cornelius had not met Hendriek on his own coming from the farm, and he had not noticed anything as it was already so dark. From there both went to the home of a boy Ole knew to be a good friend of Hendriek's, only to learn that Hendriek had been to school then left for home at dismissal when it had still been light.

From there Ole had no choice but to knock on the Sheriff's door. Trying to keep the heavy foreboding at bay, he and Cornelius rode the distance to the home of the local law enforcement and there stated his concern. Looking in Ole's eyes the sheriff didn't say anything about waiting for daylight, but swiftly bundled himself against the cold, all the while asking questions determining how and where to begin the search. Both men agreed lanterns were needed, and they would follow Hendriek's usual route from school. Two other men joined carrying lanterns and soon all were walking the short cut path to the wood bridge with no rails. At the bridge, holding the lanterns close to the wood as well as the edges, marks could be seen that appeared made by a horse struggling. And at the edge near the center of the bridge a piece of wood was splintered and gouged. One of the men stretched out on his stomach holding his lantern down as far as he could, and directly below could be seen a great hole in the ice with swift waters reflecting back light. All was silence. Daylight would show no sign of any disturbance of the snow around the gaping hole in the ice. But that night not a man there ever forgot the terrible sound that came from Ole. It was March 25th and Hendriek's body was not found until the spring thaw.

How changed everything felt. Coming to terms with what had happened didn't seem possible. The beloved son, brother, friend was apparently dead. But there could be no funeral until Hendriek's body was recovered. Each day with no closure felt like a day of torture. Neighbors shed tears of sympathy but were confused about the usual custom of bringing food for the bereaved since there was no funeral.

The happy-go-lucky Olga vanished, hiding in her room, red-eyed, refusing to talk. If she hadn't been sick; if she had been riding with him, she believed he would not have died.

Lena moved about like automation, going through the motions that looked normal, but held no meaning. She and Hendriek had been only one year apart in age and were best friends. There had never been dissention or squabbling between them. Now there was a great un-fillable emptiness in her soul.

Ole and Karen seemed broken. And Cornelius saw to the needs of the farm in silence, while the sympathetic community sporadically came with food, quietly supportive. And the church friends and pastor came offering comfort and compassion. Gradually, when the funeral was finally completed, the grieving family got back up and began putting itself back together again as best they could knowing nothing would ever be the same. But unspoken was the wondering of what had happened, that a gentle horse used to crossing the plank bridge would suddenly be wild with fear as seemed to be evidenced by the damage to the bridge.

1898

A TIME TO BREAK DOWN
AND A TIME TO BUILD UP

January: A New Year for new beginnings. But it was a heavy sadness that pervasively hung over the Hogenson family. There was almost a feeling of resistance to moving on without Hendriek. It felt like a betrayal in some odd way. Lena found comfort in her walks and talks with Lars, grateful to be able to share her feelings with him. He was an attentive listener and seemed to find words that comforted her.

By mid-April, Lars asked Lena to marry him--he had cleared the first hurdle by having a talk with Ole and gratefully received the blessing of Lena's parents. Now he wrapped his arms around Lena, holding her close, and talk of a wedding date became central.

For the first time in months Lena felt the return of joy. Smiling now, she reached for the thin ribbon about her neck and drew out the ring. Slipping the ribbon over her head, he helped loosen the knot and the ring dropped into his hand. With the ring between two fingers, and smiling broadly, he held her left hand and slipped the ring on her finger, where they both gazed in happiness. Lars whispered, "I love you, Lena", and lifting her hand sealed his sentiment with a lingering kiss on the hand of his future bride. In looking down again to the ring he paused, then gently touched the luminous green gem. It moved ever so slightly. The stone would need re-setting before the wedding. Regretfully, Lena removed the ring, and Lars wrapped it in his handkerchief, then put it in his pocket. They walked slowly, going over plans--both excited, happy, and eager to move ahead. They agreed it should be a simple church wedding considering all the family had gone through. June was chosen as flowers would be in abundance then and could be used to decorate the church. Lars told her of a small house in town that needed some fixing up, but had an appeal he liked, and wanted her opinion. With glowing faces the happy couple informed both sets of parents of the coming June wedding. Preparations for the big day were underway and it was as if skies were blue again, and the sun felt warm and one could hear bird song again after a long dark storm.

Olga went with Lena to tour the small house where Lars anxiously waited; and their response was all he could have hoped for. Though, truth-be-told, as happy as Lena was it could have been a hovel with a dirt floor and it would have seemed perfectly lovely.

In the Hogenson household Lena's hope chest was inventoried. As a well brought up daughter she had learned from an early age the skills of sewing, embroidery, and her favorite--hardanger, as well as lace making. She had a large trunk of lovely handwork. Her wedding dress was practical. A lovely pale blue-green silk with delicate lace inserts and fitted sleeves. It was good for everyone to have the happy wedding to look forward to. Good for everyone but Cornelius. He was skilled at hiding his feelings, but inwardly he raged. He threw himself into the farm work, burning off the anger trying to keep from even looking in the direction of the attractive couple as they came and went making their plans.

Lars had come across an old kitchen table which he refinished and re-glued, as well as four wooden chairs. None matched, but once refinished, glued, and stained to match the table, they were something to admire. By the time June arrived the little house was ready to be moved into, and Lars was camping there as he worked on his list of projects still to be dealt with. June 6th was the date chosen for the wedding.

Late afternoon of the 5th the wedding party met in the church to go over the ceremony, after which all would enjoy a meal in the fellowship hall in the basement of the Highland Prairie Church. The ladies had outdone themselves with flowers, ribbon, and greenery. Everything was in readiness. Such laughter and camaraderie among the young friends as they arrived--except Lars. Lena hadn't seen or heard from him all day which hadn't puzzled her until now. That he was late was odd, to say the least, and the teasing about that fact was not particularly funny to her. The minister at last quietly asked one young man who was to usher guests at the ceremony to please seek out the whereabouts of the missing groom-to-be. After a pleasant thirty minutes of light-hearted visiting the wedding party was assembled under the directions of the minister and the group of friends was put through their paces to his satisfaction. Once again there was a short wait in hopes Lars would appear. But then, there was nothing more to do but quietly file to the basement where nothing had been spared for a wonderful rehearsal meal. Lena was unable to swallow what she put in her mouth and could only push the food about her plate. Olga hung close to Lena when the quiet meal was over, and the two sets of parents conversed in low tones.

When at last the young usher returned, it was to slowly approach the couple's parents, glancing nervously at Lena, who rose swiftly and joined him as he reached Ole and Karen. What he had to say was odd, and nothing made sense to her. Lars was gone. His luggage and best clothes were gone. His personal items were gone; and so was his horse. Lars' mother fainted. Lena's knees buckled and her father put her on a chair, and she leaned her head over her knees. Karen tried to shelter her daughter in her arms, and it was Olga who burst into heart-breaking tears. Chaos reigned.

In 24 hours no evidence of preparation for a wedding could be found, and Lena had shut herself in Hendriek's former bedroom unable to talk even to her parents.

Ole stormed over to the Henderson home where loud acrimonious voices were plainly heard by neighbors who notified the law, fearing a breakout of violence. No explanation was ever forth coming, but Lars' weeping mother kept repeating, "Something's wrong! He would not do this! Never, never!" The local law washed their hands of the matter saying, "The young man simply got cold feet." And since his horse was found standing at the train depot in a near, but larger town, he was said to have boarded the train and was now, no doubt, in Chicago. This, the ticket master refuted saying, "No young fella came through here in the past 24 hours." To which the locals who collected in the town's saloon reckoned the run-away groom had saved his cash and simply ridden the train out of town in the same manner as the many hobos living hand-to-mouth along the rails. And that's how the matter was left.

Lars was out of the picture but Lena's shame and humiliation was only beginning. The worst of her suffering was from his betrayal. She loved him deeply and had believed him when he said he loved her. Somewhere in the depths of her heart she still believed he loved her; and she knew also she could never forgive him. She no longer wanted to go out in public. She could feel the pitying eyes on her, and saw the whispering behind hands. And she knew from the wondering looks they were thinking, "What did she do to drive him off like that?!" So Lena stayed at home except for church, though that, too, was torture. She struggled in her faith and was unable to pray. She lost sleep, lost weight, grew silent--speaking only when spoken to. She clung to the belief she had been loved by Lars, there was no doubt, and their love had been genuine. His mother was right--this cowardly betrayal was not in his nature. But then the darkness of it all would return in its pain, and shame, and in her misery she raged against him until she had no choice but to purge all thoughts of him, burying the sweet memories so deep they seemed gone. And there they froze.

Gone was the joy she'd felt on waking each morning. Now when her eyes opened in the early dawn, she rose and prepared for the workday setting a pattern for the rest of her life. She welcomed hard work as it would give her sleep at night. The dark hours of the night were her enemy when sleeplessness ruled.

One evening in September Olga had come into Lena's room where she had taken to retreating when work was over for the day, and the evening meal done, and things restored to order. Lena was oblivious of Cornelius most of the time, and sometimes was unaware he'd spoken to her.

This night, Olga had stepped quietly into her room and with sad eyes surveyed her sister. Closing the door and moving close to Lena, she whispered, "Lars' house burned down last night, Lena. Someone set it on fire." Ripples of shock passed over Lena, then a wave of grief. Everything truly was over. There was nothing to say. A while later she realized Olga had left.

Days became weeks. Weeks became months, and Lena depended on the routine of her daily work to find a purpose to her life.

Cornelius watched, waiting.

The hatching and care of tiny chicks was one of Lena's favorite things to do, and she was good at it, as attested to by the Hogenson henhouse and chicken coop. There were always baby chicks to sell as well as eggs. She was scrupulous in the care and provision for them--no easy task as a henhouse was ever in need of a cleaning. It was a job nobody wanted. Ever.

Cornelius made excuses to approach and talk and offer to do the cleaning but made little progress as she rejected help and preferred to work in silence. But he had convinced Ole of the practicality of putting a small heater in the bunk room. It was a simple procedure done by the two men. And the fuel was paid for out of what Cornelius had been paying his two landladies; and he even had a little of the rent money left over.

The ladies were sorry to see him leave as he had been a good boarder--clean and decent. They weren't always so lucky. And as he left, they assured him he was always welcome to rent again should the need arise.

The ladies had also come to terms in parting with the piano. It would not be needed now as there were no students. Amelia, the eldest, who had done the teaching was failing in mind and eyesight, and it was now no use to them. They hoped it would be an instrument of enjoyment to the Hogenson girls.

Ole, Cornelius and two of Hendriek's former classmates moved the cumbersome load carefully to its new home in Karen and Ole's parlor. Not an easy job with horses and rough roads. The horseless carriages were all the rage in big cities as paved streets were everywhere there. Out in the countryside they were not at all common—yet. But how the horseless carriages terrified the horses when one did come noisily through, causing some serious accidents and injuries. Cornelius was younger than Ole but neither he nor Ole ever learned to drive or owned a "flivver!"

The piano looked very grand in the parlor, but for Lena it was depressing. She no longer sang in the choir nor did she feel any urge to play the songs she loved. She knew Olga certainly had no interest, so she exerted no pressure on the girl to do what Karen was encouraging her to do--learn to play the piano. And Olga would have simply brushed away her mother's efforts to conform her, except for one thing--her overwhelming need to see her beloved sister smile and laugh again. She remembered Lena's love of music, her wonderful singing, and how happy she'd been with the piano lessons. So Olga made a deal. Lessons—only if Lena-taught-her!

Reluctantly, half-heartedly, Lena sat down on the bench

seat next to the tender-hearted Olga and began to teach. She was a born teacher. And though Olga learned to play the piano--and to do it quite well--she never had the passion for it that Lena did. During the lesson times in the following spring, Karen would pour herself a cup of coffee and sitting at her kitchen table, listen to her daughters at the piano and give thanks to Almighty God for His blessings. Olga taught Lena to laugh again, as Lena taught Olga the music she herself loved. Together the girls learned duets and sang harmony to the beautiful hymns. As spring warmed and the windows were opened, Ole and Cornelius listened as the laughter and music floated out into the sunshine. Both men were filled with hope. Very different hopes.

Cornelius had talked frequently, of late, to Ole about raising a few pigs. He knew Ole disliked pigs, but he, himself had always had an affinity for them and would like to see a few on the Hogenson farm. And ham was so good! A nice change from chicken, lamb, and beef. Now sheep Cornelius hated--they were stupid as well as too much trouble. Pigs were so much easier, as well as tastier. So Ole agreed to maybe two. The men worked well together, and Ole was grateful for the strong, sober Cornelius who had come to be regarded by the girls as a youngish uncle or an older cousin, while to Ole and Karen he was like a member of the family. And under his placid exterior, Cornelius chafed in frustration at un-fulfillment of his cherished dreams.

Lena still avoided going out much but did join a quilting group of mostly older women, but also some closer to her age, and soon learned to put together beautiful quilts using very fine stitching, earning accolades from the older women. The feel of the fabric between her fingers took her mind to pleasanter places, and she was never without her sewing basket filled with her sharp shears, all colors of embroidery floss, hoops, crochet needles and thread.

Then she began making Olga's school dresses--and Olga

became the envy of every girl in town. Each day that passed Lena formed a new life for herself. Marriage did not interest her. Her father was the only man she trusted. A part of her heart was ice. The newspapers wrote things that filled her mind, and she wished she could transport herself to the cities, and places where the suffragettes were marching for voting rights for women. A part of her mind told her men were not better than women--that there was a terrible injustice here. She wished she could do something worthwhile. The women's voting rights did on occasion come up at the supper table, which her mother always remained silent on, as was Cornelius, but she saw the muscles in his cheeks as his jaw clenched and knew him to be irritated. Olga cheered for the women and was ready to march, while Ole would thoughtfully say, "Some things need to change, yah. But this does not look like a good way to me. In time, maybe things get better."

In her room at night Lena read her Bible, going over Sunday's Scripture verses, and thinking over the minister's sermon. She wanted to be able to pray again, but she could not forgive Lars for his betrayal, and thus felt she could not pray to God with such anger and unforgiveness in her heart. These were feelings and thoughts she could share with no one. The path forward for her life remained hidden. She was grateful her parents put no pressure on her, nor did they criticize her in her reluctance to socialize with her young friends as she had in the past. As she became more content in the quiet withdrawn existence she had slipped into, her parents became worried. They talked quietly in the dark of night in their bed when no one could hear or interrupt. Olga also was part of their concern as they watched her follow in Lena's footsteps, beginning to assimilate her ways as Lena drifted day-by-day toward spinsterhood.

Indeed, it frightened Karen and Ole. They knew full well the desperate circumstances of widows and unmarried women. Unless there was a husband, they existed in poverty, and as with the spinster landladies, their end was soon to be in the poor house--a fate considered worse than death. It was now almost two years since the disastrous day of the wedding rehearsal, and Ole dreaded the day when he knew he would have to push Lena out of the nest, so to speak. In time the farm would be divided between the two girls, but the running of it, or managing it, in his mind, clearly required a man. Lena was 21 and already being referred to as an old maid. Her classmates had all married. The anxious parents agreed to leave things as they were for a few more months, but then something must be said.

Cornelius had recently returned from a holiday with his parents and Belle. It had been a pleasant interlude as usual. It was always good being back in the bosom of his welcoming family. While he was there, he'd gone the three miles to Mabel to see again the farm west of the town about three-quarter of a mile. The elderly couple had died, and the son, in poor health, needed to let the farm go. Cornelius had his farm! Now he would need to have the talk with Ole that was the second part of his long-held dream: Lena

He took his time arranging his thoughts, carefully preparing what, and how, to say all that he needed to say in a way to promote his request--which was permission to court Lena in the hopes of marriage.

He went about the usual farm work, thinking and planning after the visit to Hesper and Mabel. He would need to stay long enough to find an acceptable hired hand for Ole. Contented now, pleased with how things seemed to be falling into place, he pitched bedding straw to the floor of the barn, and uncovered a nest of kittens. Then one by one he snapped their necks and carried the limp bodies out to the pigs.

1900

A TIME TO WEEP AND
A TIME TO LAUGH

C. Erickson Farm Home, circa 1935

The first Sunday following the visit to his parent's home, Cornelius approached his friend and employer after church with quiet dignity and requested if he might have a serious, private conversation with Ole at his convenience. Taken aback, he searched Cornelius' face for several seconds before asking if a meeting at the house was preferred, or somewhere more private. "More private," was the answer. Puzzled, Ole asked, "The bunkhouse, perhaps?" "Yes, sir. That would be preferred," was Cornelius' respectful reply.

Cornelius could feel perspiration beading on his face beginning to trickle from his hairline as he stood facing his puzzled employer. He wished he'd thought to bring in a second chair so they could be seated for the stressful conversation soon to begin. Too late for chairs now. Trying to bring some semblance of calm to his thoughts he concentrated on knowing that he and Ole were good friends with mutual respect. Pulling out a clean handkerchief he slowly dried his forehead and began his well-rehearsed speech. "Ole, it's been five years I've been working here and you know what kind of a man I am. If anyone knows me well, that would be you. For me, it's an honor to call you my friend. You know my work. You know I have my own farm now; that I work hard and can support a wife and family. This has been my goal for years. I am asking your permission to court Olena with hopes of marriage, God-willing. You know I am a non-violent man and she would come to no harm through me." Cornelius felt as though he had cotton in his mouth from the long speech, and now trailed into silence. Inwardly, he was churning, hating the sound of his own voice. Now he waited for Ole's response as he tried to assess what it would be from what looked like shock on his employer's face.

It took Ole a few seconds to absorb all he had just heard from Cornelius—and he wondered why he had never been aware of his hired hand having feelings like this for Lena. So his first question was, "When did you know you felt this way about Lena?"

To Cornelius' credit, he was honest with the fact he had always loved Olena, but a poor man with nothing to offer a woman should keep his feelings to himself.

Cornelius assured Ole that he could now offer a good home and support to wife and children, should they be so blessed. Cornelius had pulled out all the stops, and felt relief loosening tight muscles when he saw agreement in Ole's face along with a small nod of his head. Hope returned.

Ole, though, turned very serious and seemed deep in thought for what seemed too long to Cornelius. But when he spoke, Ole sounded sad. Looking closely at Cornelius he was speaking as a loving father when he told him, "This has to be Lena's decision. She has been through so much and is so changed. At times I hardly know her. I will need time to think on this myself, Cornelius. A little more time. I will talk more on this with you—I was not aware of any of what you have told me concerning Lena."

As Ole left the bunkroom, Cornelius breathed a sigh of relief and wiped his brow one more time. Waiting for the response would not be easy. Cornelius took a few more minutes to collect his thoughts following the stressful meeting. Resentment had risen in his heart and mind, that things should be so hard for him, while it had appeared so easy for Ole's children to be looking forward to eventually stepping into Ole's shoes and having the ownership of such a perfect farm. For a brief moment Hendriek cast a shadow over Cornelius' mind, but he pushed the thoughts aside. The farm would some day be Lena's and Olga's. Why did he have to work so hard for every little thing he longed for? And what would Lena or Olga know about the running of the farm? Who knows, maybe someday, Ole's farm would be his! The thought brought a lift to Cornelius' mood.

Chores that evening took slightly more time than normal, though nothing of the conversations was forthcoming at the evening meal, but Ole was distracted, and Cornelius quieter than usual. But the talk was of the latest in politics, and major events. President McKinley was going to be running for a second term--and bound to get it after the end of the Spanish-American war had resulted in the defeated Spain, giving to the U.S. the Philippines, and Guam, and Puerto Rico. McKinley was a much-loved man by all who met him. Less popular table talk was of the marching of the suffragettes in the cities in their struggle for the right to vote. Lena and Olga held very strong opinions on the subject.

Ole continued to mull over Sunday's conversation for several more days before informing Cornelius he would discuss the matter with Karen and then they could talk further. To rush things would not be beneficial.

Later as the couple lay in their bed, talking in low tones, they agreed to let Lena know of Cornelius' marriage proposal, but to exert no pressure on her. It must be her decision. The time chosen for the talk was to be when Olga had gone off to school. Olga now walked to the end of their lane and was picked up by a neighbor's child in a small pony cart.

With breakfast over, and Olga out the door, Cornelius left to begin chores, but Ole poured himself another cup of coffee as Karen folded her fingers together in a tight nervous grip. Lena paused in clearing the table, looking in confusion at the oddness of her parent's actions. Clearing his throat, Ole touched a chairback and indicated for Lena to sit. And, as she sat down, her mother took a chair beside her, and Ole began to speak. "If there is one thing I know, Lena, it is that pain is part of living. I am sorry for all you have suffered—for no fault of your own; the unfairness of it all. And I know you are as aware as your mother and I are of the unfair treatment and lack of opportunities for women in a world run by men. I understand that. I cannot change that. Mother and I would fail you if we did not do all we could to help you towards a good and secure life with a chance at happiness. All I ask is that you hear me out and keep an open mind to what I say to you for your own good. We will respect your decision." Ole paused for a much-needed mental rest to put Cornelius' request into the best light as possible. He didn't know if it was possible. "What I present to you now your mother and I have carefully thought about and discussed. I have been respectfully approached by Cornelius requesting permission to court you. He professes love of long standing for you but could not pursue until he knew he could offer you a good home and life equal to what you have. It is our hope you will consider this proposal fairly and respectfully, and give Cornelius your answer."

She was so still it seemed she didn't breathe; color left her face, then lifting sad blue eyes, regretfully informed her parents she had no desire to marry anyone. Ever. And she would leave it to her father to so inform Cornelius. Ole spoke again saying she needed to think about this seriously. Certainly, this was a surprise, and of course she could take her time and after due consideration, give her answer. Before she could respond to that he left without looking back.

Cornelius must have been waiting for him, for he met Ole just inside the barn door, unasked questions plain to see on his face.

"The decision is Lena's to make. Give her time to think things through." That it might be days--many days--before there was an answer was not totally unexpected by Cornelius, but he was still disappointed. The men talked of the eventual departure of Cornelius, and the need to begin the search for a good dependable replacement. They would have to get the word out in town as soon as possible.

In the kitchen Lena, unsmiling, looked steadily at her mother until Karen had to look away. Then in an empty voice she asked, "Is this what you and Father discuss so late in the night? Me? What to do with me? Do you want me gone so badly you'd give me away?"

Then Karen cried, tears falling from her cheeks to the bib of her apron. "No--no--no! Of course not! But what choice is there for a woman? How can you support yourself? We won't always be here, and this farm is Olga's as well as yours! We want you safe. That is all! And to have your own family. Please, please, Olena--think on this--it is for your own good." But Karen's weeping wouldn't stop. In her heart of hearts she knew Lena didn't, and never would, love Cornelius. And she felt as though her own heart was breaking. Her beautiful, intelligent daughter deserved so much more. And mixed in was fury, aimed at Lars--the betrayer! Liar!

Whatever further thinking was going on in Lena's head, that was where it stayed. The lengths of her silence grew longer. Any further mealtime chatter ended and she ate her meal in silence seated across from a man who meant nothing to her, who had now proposed marriage to her through her parents. She was repelled and desired nothing so much as to know the man had been replaced with a new hired hand, and she would never see Cornelius again.

When Olga had been informed of the situation on her return home from school that first day, she was sternly warned to say nothing, to not meddle; to mind her own business. And Olga promptly proceeded to do the opposite. The uproar the loyal Olga made stressed her parents to the limits and she was banned to her bedroom to eat her meals in solitude until such time as she controlled herself.

It did have the brief and welcome moment of making Lena laugh out loud; and then giving her sister a grateful hug.

The days passed into weeks and still she said nothing. Karen, in despair, begged Ole to let the whole matter die. Soon Cornelius would be gone. Three men had come about the job and it seemed an easy choice as all were local and experienced in farm work. But Ole felt differently. Especially since Cornelius now had his own farm and home. He was a hard worker and would be a good provider, and was by the grace of God, a teetotaler. Lena would be well-cared for; and that was foremost to Ole.

The day came when Ole put down his work out on the farm and returned to the house. He found Lena in the kitchen with her hands and wrists buried in a large pan of bread dough, punching it down so it could rise once more, off to the side of the cook stove, over the warm water reservoir. In a firm, steady voice, putting a hand on her shoulder to turn her to face him, he gently placed his other hand on the other shoulder--he told her--"It is time, Lena. You are being offered a safe, secure home for yourself and for your children, God-willing. It is time to move on. And it is time to be respectful to Cornelius and give him his answer." With that he kissed his daughter's golden hair, and turning, went back to his work. Karen had listened with an aching heart. It was out of her hands. But she never got over the regrets that plagued her for not putting up a fight for her daughter's happiness.

Lena did not sleep that night. She lay motionless on her bed, staring up at the dark ceiling, seeing nothing. She tried to envision living with Cornelius, sharing the same house, the same bed, sitting across from him every meal, every day, forever--and that was when the tears flowed, and heart-rending sobs could no longer be held back. She told herself many marriages were arranged and turned out to be successful--but still she sobbed. And in the adjoining room, a loyal young sister sobbed also.

Morning came and two tired red-eyed girls ate an early breakfast alone and were out of the kitchen by the time the men came in for breakfast. Karen silently placed the big country breakfast in front of the men with no explanation for the girls' absence, and Ole turned his attention to his food without comment.

Olga dragged herself off to school after leveling a scowl in her mother's direction. When she was safely out of the house, Lena appeared in the kitchen again, and sat down at the table, waiting till her mother was seated across from her. After what seemed like long minutes, their eyes met. Karen's troubled and unhappy, Lena's empty. To Karen's shock she heard what sounded like a laugh come from Lena's stiff face. Then again— louder and unpleasant, followed by an almost disbelieving, slightly mocking, "What a ridiculous pair we will look! I am a half a head taller than he is."

Shocked, Karen heard herself saying, "You weren't raised to speak disrespectfully of others. We are all made as God intended."

Slowly, Lena rose and turned to leave the kitchen, but pausing at the door she spoke again in a listless voice, "Tell Father I will do as you and he have asked. After all who else would ever want me?" And the horrid, ironic laugh came again.

Cornelius and Olena Erickson, circa 1900

With a decision arrived at, and Cornelius having received his answer from Olena, marriage plans moved swiftly and June 20th was chosen for the small wedding which would be held in the Hesper Lutheran church with Lena wearing her mother's wedding dress. Photographs were taken of the couple; one of the bride sitting and the groom standing, one of the bride standing and the groom sitting, but none of both standing as the bride towered over the groom as evidenced in the one photo of both seated. And all expressions so serious, with no smiles. There was no honeymoon and the couple moved into the big Victorian house set on the top of the high hill. All Lena carried with her was her personal effects and clothing. Some household furniture was bought with the purchase of the farm: the iron wood burning range in the kitchen as well as the table and chairs. A heavy oak library table and leather cushioned oak rocker in the living room and a pot belly coal burning stove. A brass double-bed was left in the master bedroom, which had a walk-in dressing room closet--the only closet in a house with seven bedrooms. Lena set her mind to be as positive in spirit as possible with the help of Almighty God.

Cornelius at 38 was set in his ways, a man not given to considering the needs or feelings of anyone other than himself, and it would have been a kindness to womankind had he continued a bachelor. He did not take well any suggestion for change in himself, though he expected Lena to change for him. This aspect of his personality was fixed, while his belief that a wife was comparable to a mare which only needed to be trained well, did not bode well for a happy union for either partner.

Once the decision for marriage to Cornelius had been resolved in her mind, Lena set her will to live as she had been taught: whatever your task, work heartily, as serving the Lord, not men! Colossians 3:23. Lena knew her Bible. When her mother, who married just before sailing for America, had put in the one trunk she could bring, the large family Bible filled with family records, she knew what she wanted her family to learn and live by. And she had also carefully packed her wedding dress. Now Lena vowed to herself she would be the best that she could be and hoped, in time, the bitterness would be forgotten.

Lena's Mother's Family Bibelen

So much had been packed into the days just before and then after the wedding, it was hard to process it all. Cornelius' parents, Hans and Maren, and sisters, Belle and Carrie had welcomed Lena warmly and sincerely when she arrived at the Erikson farm near Hesper, where she dressed for the small and private wedding in the little country church. Their friendship was real and lasted their lifetimes--so needed and cherished by Lena.

The farmland Cornelius now owned had been rented out

to a neighbor for the past five-plus years by the ailing owners. He would receive the rent until the next planting season when he could work his own land. In the meantime he purchased a milk cow and piglets.

Parents of the newlyweds, as well as Lena's sister-in-law Carrie, were generous with extra pots, pans, dishes, flatware, lamps, and bedding. The large house was mostly empty but was still functional. Money was not plentiful, but at least adequate for a hard-working couple.

And the work commenced from the first day of life together in the big house on a modest farm overlooking the small town of Mabel. Respectable society centered always around church and family. No surprise the new Mr. and Mrs. Cornelius Erickson attended faithfully at the 1st Evangelical Lutheran Church in Mabel. And three miles south, Hans and Maren attended the same denomination in Hesper. Carrie, and her husband Chris, lived eight miles west of Mabel in Prosper, Minnesota. In the following days and weeks Lena's new in-laws lovingly and happily came to assist her in setting up her own new home. Maren couldn't see well enough to help but wouldn't have missed the camaraderie for anything. Olga and Karen arrived and all, but Maren, scrubbed, cleaned, and improvised; and the big echoing house lit with sun streaming in sparkling windows--though no curtains yet. Floors were mopped, walls wiped down; rag-rugs appeared and were placed at entrances to catch dirt and debris. The water reservoir was scrubbed out, and refilled; the stove polished.

Cornelius filled the attached shed on the north end of the house with split firewood he'd purchased. A white enamel bucket was filled with well water pumped up by the windmill by the barn and placed on the built-in green counter in the large pantry. A white enamel dipper hung from the side of the pail.

A black enamel bucket was tucked out of sight between the wood range and the wall in the winter kitchen for wastewater. This was where cooking and eating was done. The large summer kitchen was between the main kitchen and woodshed, and was used for canning, baking and summer cooking to keep the heat down in the house in the summer. A wood range had been left there by the former occupants. Lena thought the rambling house was charming and felt grateful that it was hers to turn into a home. And passing through her memory came the verse, "Continue steadfastly in prayer, being watchful in it with Thanksgiving!" By the door in the summer kitchen, an old washstand, with a cut-out for a large basin, had been placed, with a big pitcher of water. Towels hung from a rod on each end, and a bar of soap lay in a white oval dish. Here the men washed up as they came in for meals and after work. Another large black pail sat waiting for wastewater beside the washstand. Pegs were on the wall on the other side of the door for outdoor clothing; and an old rag-rug lay beneath for boots and over-shoes. The walls throughout the house were bare of decorations. Karen and Olga had brought along Lena's hope chest that she had purposely left behind with all its memories. She didn't want to be reminded of the happy days turned to ashes, but said nothing and had the trunk put to the back of the walk-in dressing/bathing room. Where it was to remain, undisturbed. Cornelius stored his locked sailor's desk box on a top shelf inside the room's wide doorway. A window lit up the dressing room every morning as the sun rose.

Every Sunday morning Lena and Cornelius were the picture of respectability entering church. Cornelius liked showing Lena off and he liked walking her towards the front seats. If Lena had hoped to leave behind the staring and gossip, nothing had changed except now it was for a different reason. People's heads did turn to see a short, stocky, ordinary older man with such a beautiful wife. She wasn't just taller than her husband, she was much taller, and adding to the difference was the big hat that was the custom. All the ladies covered their heads in church.

It would not be long before the preacher would make a house call and he would have to be received in the living room, as the adjoining parlor, with its piano room, was totally empty; its only attraction was the south-facing picture window with its border of stained glass, while the window in the door leading to the long open porch boasted the same ruby, blue and gold stained glass. It was an inviting room. The stairs to the six bedrooms led upwards between living room and parlor. In the not too distant future, a grandfather clock would stand at the base of the stairs where for a lifetime it would toll each hour of the day and night, its deep throated "bong" reaching into every bedroom in the house, many times waking a restless sleeper, and then keep them informed of their fleeing hours of sleep. Cornelius would become the winder, and the keeper, of the clock with the key always in his possession. He would be the one to keep the wood range going into the late night, and have it going for Lena to make breakfast, and the water warm for washing in. A washstand had been acquired for the bedroom with the usual pitcher and basin. Outside, hidden behind lilac bushes on this end of the house was the two-seater outhouse where no one wanted to run out to in the dark of night, so hidden under the brass bed was a lidded receptacle, humorously called a "thunder-mug". Everything seemed to be coming together that was needed for a smooth- running existence.

Lena had already learned to leave well enough alone in respect to the smelly pipe. Cornelius would smoke where he wished, his tobacco safely locked in his box-desk in the closet. And Lena would have to turn her head away from the smell of his breath in the night. She had grown up on a farm and was not lacking in understanding reproductive process. When Lena had done as her father advised her in considering what would be for her a loveless marriage to Cornelius, the only factor that presented in favor of the union was a desire to have a family of her own. So she submitted as was expected of her, asking nothing, expecting nothing. As long as her husband was satisfied things went smoothly. If she objected, life did not go so pleasantly—so she became accommodating for the sake of peace. He told her he had always loved her, but his constant demands on her did not feel loving, especially when an occasional "No" made him angry. Which invariably was followed up with some form of punishment—mental or emotional, never physical. Cornelius also had no interest in discussing any issues between them. He was adept at turning any attempt on Lena's part to talk things out into personal attacks on him—even calling her a "controlling nag". Silent accommodation appeared to be all he really wanted. Lena felt like a useful, but mindless, possession. Divorce was, simply put, not done. Separation for a woman was out of the question. The beginning of depression had begun.

Cornelius had taken on the replenishing of reservoir water and drinking water, as well as filling the wood box and the coal scuttle in the small windowless room in the living room. He also used these duties to teach Lena the rules of his household by withholding the fulfillment of one, sometimes more, of the duties. And Lena learned to go along for the sake of peace, assessing what was worth fighting for and what to let go.

When pullets were available, Cornelius came home with two dozen for Lena to care for. He hadn't asked her, which hadn't surprised her as he'd been busy getting the chicken coop mended and cleaned. When he unloaded chicken feed and watering pans, she knew it would not be long. When he showed up with two dozen agitated pullets for her to care for, she was mixing up her bread for the week--not a good time. He was impatient but had to wait until the bread was ready to set aside to rise. She didn't say anything but set about dealing with the nervous creatures. Chickens she understood, and liked. Not the cleaning of their living quarters though--they were dirty. Now she looked after them, filling their feed pans, and water containers before slowly letting them out of their cages to calm down; to eat and drink. They would become accustomed to her care.

With the garden, things went a little differently. Not only did she dislike being taken for granted, but it was probably her aching back that made her less cooperative.

It was laundry day and doing the laundry was neither simple nor easy. It was heavy work hauling in pails full of water to be brought to boiling on the wood range in the summer kitchen. Cornelius carried the water in and carried it out again when the washing was done. It was a job he hated, but which he did in silence--until his sons were big enough to do the despised job. Lena had two large wash tubs set on improvised supports consisting of sturdy boards on sawhorses. One tub was filled with cold water, the other with the boiling water scooped carefully with a large pan. Scalding was not unheard of. All of the sorting of the laundry was done while the heating took place, and then Lena began the process of shaving slivers of Fels Naptha Bar Soap into the tub for the hot water. Lena was familiar with the popular laundry bar through her mother's use of it from 1893. But at this point, the real work begins with placing the load of whites into the hot, soapy water and sloshing around, back and forth, up and down with the use of the laundry stick, an approximately two feet long smoothed stick with no sharp edges to damage material. Then one by one with the stick, each piece is lifted to a scrub board where any stubborn stains are laboriously scrubbed by hand, with more use of the remnant bar of soap. Lena's hands became rough and work worn. Winter laundry days were the worst when her fingers and knuckles cracked and bled. And the wringing of the pieces was difficult--necessary prior to the rinse and again afterwards. Cornelius eventually purchased a hand crank two-roller wringer that clamped on the tub rim, making things easier for Lena in the laundry realm, but for now she struggled with sore hands and painful back. When she hung the first batch on the line, she saw Cornelius had plowed the garden with a horse pulling the garden plow. She was finishing the second batch when he walked in carrying bags of vegetable seeds to be planted. "These need planting. Going to rain tomorrow or next day, so these need to be gotten in the ground."

She knew she sounded snappy, but in that moment didn't care, " I can't stop in the middle of this!"

And he had snapped back, "That can wait, this can't." He wasn't pleased to hear her say, "You'll have to help me!" but he did set the twine line rows.

And that was the day she used Cornelius methods of punishment against him. She cut six inches of her hair off. He couldn't keep his hands out of her hair, unbraiding it at night, stroking it; it excited him. It didn't matter to him that it was easier to manage in the morning left in a braid. The tangles and knots were painful and time-consuming. She had begun to hate her hair.

His fury over cutting her hair had frightened her, but she stood her ground, making him listen as she told him of her exhaustion, her aching back, and that her hair was hers to do with as she wished, or needed. He'd certainly ignored her suggestion to shave his mustache.

Turning his back on her, he put the lamp out, letting her find her way in the dark. At least he left her alone.

Adjusting to married life wasn't easy for either of them. There were days when Cornelius wondered what he'd gotten himself into. It had taken five long years to finally claim the object of his obsession, only to realize Lena did not, and would not love him! She would give only what was required of a dutiful wife. When she turned her face away from him at night, he remembered her arms around Lars; how they walked and talked and laughed. Now she rarely smiled, and only talked where needed. She worked hard in her home. It simply did not occur to him that his breath was unpleasant, and a mustache could be repelling to some women. He was set to stay as he was.

He wasn't surprised when in February Lena told him she thought she might be pregnant, but he hoped she was mistaken. In March she repeated what she suspected, saying some time in September the baby would be born. He did not feel overjoyed. It was a responsibility he did not particularly want. And he did not find the physical changes in Lena appealing. He made fast exits when the morning sickness started –some things he felt he did not need to see.

As the pregnancy progressed, Lena needed more help in some of her work so he'd asked her if Olga could come for the summer to help around the house and garden--and maybe the chickens? At 17, Olga had one more year of school, and the boisterous girl tormented her parents with her talk of the big cities, and the women's movement for equality, and she laughingly insisted that was exactly where she was going to go to join the marches. Lena missed her upbeat, fun-loving sister, and agreed she did want Olga to come for the summer. Whatever room that girl walked into seemed to come alive.

June arrived and so did Olga. Cornelius was content tilling and planting his fields, away from the sounds of high-pitched female chatter, and silly laughing. At least Lena was more cheerful. Coming home dirty and tired, still having the cow to milk, he wished there was a way to have hired help. Maybe someday. In the time it took to go from barn to pig lot, his tiredness and mood lifted. He poured food and water into their trough, then cupped a hand to his mouth and made a loud, high "su-wee!" several times, and propping one foot on the low board lining the bottom of the wire fence, watched as the young pigs fast-trotted, squealing all the way, shoving and rooting each other out of the way to be first at the mess he'd poured out for them. He very much enjoyed raising swine and hoped to add to the number in time. As well as more cows.

Olga was excited for Lena and bubbling with eagerness to be the best aunt in the world to whatever little boy or girl would arrive. They discussed what names were most popular, what names they liked best. It was good for Lena to have Olga around. A cot had been borrowed and placed in the empty piano room off the parlor for Olga.

The meal was ready when Cornelius finished chores and washed up. It was kept warm on the warming shelf over the cook stove. As they waited, the girls wandered room to room of the big house, dreaming out loud of pretty furnishings. In the piano room, Olga pointed, not for the first time to an inner wall and then pretended to play the piano while she sang "Waltzing Matilda"--and once again, Lena laughed, shook her head, and turned to leave. Then stopping, she moved to the only window in the small room and watched Cornelius feeding his pigs, resting one foot on a board, smoking his pipe. She didn't speak, her thoughts her own.

Olga stood beside her and looking out she thought, "How relaxed he looks out there. Different somehow." She was unsure what she thought of her brother-in-law. She couldn't say she disliked him, but neither did she much like him. Something always just seemed "off" about him. And suddenly she thought of Hendriek--"had Hendriek felt that way towards Cornelius too? There was always something...."

Abruptly, Lena turned from the window, saying, "He'll be coming in soon now, best put everything on the table."

Back in the kitchen, Olga took up where they'd left off: the piano. Always about the piano. Olga wanted her sister to have it--so perfect for that room. But Lena showed no interest in playing it, or even singing anymore, and Olga was troubled by this change in her talented, musical sister, and kept the pressure on Lena to change her mind. Finally Olga hit on the right approach saying, "If you have a daughter, she deserves to have the chance to learn to play the piano. You must have a real music room!" And laughing, Lena finally said, "Oh, all right! You win--as usual!"

It was good to be able to just lay her tired body and aching back on her bed, sinking into the feather mattress. Oh, to sleep. But once in bed Lena's thoughts kept her restless, wondering what kind of father Cornelius would be. She knew he found her condition distasteful, unattractive. But surely, he would feel differently once he saw and held his own child in his arms.

As the weeks passed and the pregnancy became too noticeable, Lena stayed home from church; and Cornelius went without her, relieved. He slept with his back to her, keeping distance between them. The day came when he came home from the feed store with more than chicken feed.

Someone had sold him a second-hand three-quarter size rope bed that he carried up stairs to the long, narrow east-facing bedroom, and then carried up some of his clothing, and his locked desk-box. This came about after the cradle was placed in a corner of their bedroom. And now he explained to Lena that with her being up in the night feeding a crying baby, he would be unable to sleep, so it was best if he had the upstairs bedroom to go to. Once again, she worried for the baby's sake. Would he feel differently when it arrived?

Olga wanted to miss school in September declaring she could make it up. Really, she just had to be here for the new arrival, but Karen arrived by bus to escort her daughter back home, and to school.

Cornelius' Sailor's Desk Box

Karen was troubled as she watched her oldest daughter. She looked more rested and relaxed since Olga had arrived in June, but how thin Lena was; and always straightening her back. Maybe that was just the pregnancy? But there also seemed a disconnect between Lena and Cornelius. Was something wrong?--Lena was too quiet. She kept her thoughts to herself. "But," Karen thought, "people do not involve themselves in other people's private lives."

It was nice to see the baby clothes made in Lena's fine stitching. Soft flannel diapers with hand-stitched edges, bonnets, crocheted booties, gowns, and blankets. All of Karen's own children had slept in the cradle that would soon hold her first grandchild. All was in readiness.

Lena dreaded Olga's departure, and struggled against the depression she knew would return when silence would again settle over the big house. She tried to think only of the baby--babies are not quiet, they cry, yes. But they also make sweet sounds, and happy sounds. There are good changes ahead she told herself over and over, forcing herself to believe.

The feel of fine muslin in her hands helped keep her mind from going where she didn't want to dwell. She was stitching the long baptismal gown with its under-petticoat. Tiny stitches, delicate lace around such small wrist cuffs and neck edge. Tiny tucks covered the doll-sized bodice. Lena's work was exquisite. Baptism was by sprinkling the infant in the Lutheran church. It was a very important and special event, attended by family members, and recorded in the family Bible. A very important day, with family from near and far arriving at the child's home after the service.

She felt heavy and clumsy as she neared her time. Belle came often bringing Maren, and the

Baptismal Gown Handmade by Olena

meals that had always been favorites of Cornelius'. Belle was uplifting, a cheerful nurturing woman. Lena wished she could keep her wonderful sister-in-law near every day--especially now. The local doctor estimated that some time in the first ten days of September as full term. The delivery would be home birth; and all seemed in readiness as much as possible. Cornelius had resumed sleeping downstairs in case he needed to go for the doctor during the night.

Lena was restless most of the night of September 2nd, moving and shifting, at times moaning in her sleep. As daylight slowly lightened the room, Lena knew something had changed during the night. Perhaps the long wait would soon be ending. On rising she found evidence of blood, and the baby seemed so still, but otherwise, nothing seemed different.

Cornelius, aware now of what was happening, did what he could for their breakfast, but Lena left her oatmeal untouched; and soon Cornelius went to look after the animals. By mid-morning he was unnerved enough about the blood he hitched up the horse and made his way to the doctor's office where he delivered his report on Lena's progress.

Dr. Murdock looked older than his fifty years: gray-haired, tired looking. He was called out too many nights and cared deeply for all his patients. Now he reassured Cornelius it sounded like things were starting and the slight bleeding was quite normal, as was the somnolence of the fetus. He would check on Lena within the hour, but first babies took longer to birth.

So from there Cornelius made a quick visit to Hesper so Belle and Maren could prepare to come to the house. He returned to his home as quickly as he could and found the doctor there who had already checked Lena, and now knew the birthing process had indeed begun, but was not imminent. Giving the anxious couple reassurance that all was going as it should, and that he would be nearby, he then left to tend to other patients.

In the early afternoon, Hans dropped Belle and Maren off, and after having a cup of coffee, and visit with Cornelius, he left to get back to his own work. Life goes on and babies do take their time.

The doctor made another house call that evening, and in his estimation, the baby would most likely arrive after midnight. He was right.

Henry Orlando, named after Hendriek, arrived early morning on the 4th of September 1901, a perfect baby boy with thick dark hair and a good set of lungs. Cornelius leaned over his son, studying the red, angry face, listening to the furious cries--and seemed lost for words. But what he was thinking was –"I'd prefer a girl. Like Lena." As Lena prepared to nurse her son, Cornelius left the room.

Cornelius was able, and would physically care for his son, as he did for Lena, but emotionally he was incapable of nurturing anyone. He viewed his wife, and son, as extensions of himself, as being there for his needs first and foremost. Lena would try to the best of her ability to fill the void for her son that Cornelius left.

In the midst of the joy of Henry's arrival, in two days, the nation was rocked by the assassination of the beloved President McKinley.

Those of the family able to attend Henry's baptism greeted and gifted the child named after Lena's brother Hendriek. Over time other aunts and uncles met the young boy and were charmed by the bright, pleasant natured child. The doting grandparents visited as often as they could, helping him with his first steps. Teaching him words. Lena sang again, first the lullabies, then quaint children's songs, and when in church, the small boy was mesmerized by the mellow tones of the organ.

Cornelius worried the boy was becoming a sissy.

For Lena, that first year with Henry filled her with joy. Caring for him put meaning in her life.

Shortly after her son's first birthday, Lena knew she would be having a second child the following spring, and she dreaded telling Cornelius. He would not be pleased. Trying to pick the right moment to tell him never presented itself, so she simply blurted the words out as he dressed one morning before going to fire up the stove. For some seconds he didn't move, but she saw the clenching of his teeth, the tight muscles in his cheeks, and she knew he was upset, if not angry. He didn't answer, but finished tying his shoelaces, and went out to the kitchen as usual. And Lena knew nothing had changed.

Henry was trying to pull himself up by anything he could grip, and Lena knew he would be walking by the time the baby came, but he would still be in diapers. She set to work making new flannel diapers and gathered together everything Henry had outgrown. Nothing was ever thrown away. And once again Belle and Olga cheered her up and cheered her on. She loved them. They were God's bright lights in her life and she was faithful in her gratitude to God.

January of 1903 was snow on top of snow so deep it was hard to get doors open. Cornelius struggled to clear narrow tracks to the chickens, the barn, the pigs, and the outhouse. He enjoyed the good reputation of a man not given to bad language, but out in the cold, alone, unheard--he cursed the snow with every foul word he knew.

Lena was due in early April; Henry would be only 19 months old. Already, he was trying to talk, his small mouth shaping "O's" as he worked to say back what he saw was being said. Lena never baby-talked him but used simple sentences in gentle tones with her face near his. She loved looking into his dark blue eyes. And when he did eventually begin to talk it was with complete sentences. He seemed a marvel to those who met him for the first time.

The 31st of March was seemingly just another day for Lena as she looked after Henry and completed household chores as best she could. Her feet ached from the extra weight she carried, and her back just always seemed a bother. Olga had been staying with her the past week, bringing light-heartedness to almost everything. But Lena knew this backache seemed different; now it was low across the back, and the muscles felt tight. She said nothing about it, and after the evening meal was over, with everything in order, she bathed and dressed Henry for bed.

They had been given an old oval shaped oak trundle bed on four white porcelain wheels. It had canvas stretched and tacked on its underside and could be slid beneath the bed when not in use. This was Henry's bed. One he couldn't fall out of, and one that she kept by her bed. But with the need for the cradle again, the trundle was now in the parlor, close to Olga in the music room. Henry hadn't liked the change, but he loved his delightful Aunt Olga, and quickly came around, much to Lena's relief.

It took awhile to find a comfortable position, but once she did Lena slipped into a sound, restful sleep. Towards morning, as the room lightened, she woke, gratefully rested, and slipped her feet into slippers. Then, slipping her robe on, she quietly went out the living room door, which was actually a quicker way to the outhouse than through the two kitchens.

Business done, on her return, she heard a soft "poof" and felt warm slippery liquid pour down her legs, filling her slippers. Her first reaction was horror, quickly followed by gratitude that this had happened outside--and that she was coming from, and not going to, the outhouse. Now her eyes went to the window in Olga's sleeping quarters. Walking carefully, with squishing sounds coming from her slippers with every step, she tapped her knuckles lightly on the windowpane to get Olga's attention without waking Henry. In seconds, Olga was trying to raise the window, but the thing refused to budge. Signing with her hands, Olga pointed to herself--door—out.

So Lena waited until a frazzled-looking Olga rushed up to her. A swift assessment of the situation, and needs, led to Olga's fast return to the house for bath towels and a pair of dry homemade knit footies. And soon Lena was back in her bedroom where Cornelius, who was sleeping near as delivery approached, had come awake and soon knew he would be contacting the doctor before anything else this morning.

And so it was: Clarence Bernhard Erickson made his grand entrance on April Fool's Day. He was as healthy and perfect as Henry had been, but Clarence wasn't as much of a screamer, and didn't seem as furious as his older brother--though he did do some crying before calming down. And he had red hair.

This delivery had been easier, and shorter, leaving Lena not nearly as tired this time.

Cornelius had come into the bedroom when all was restored to order by Olga, and the doctor had left after shaking the father's hand and congratulating him. If he hadn't been in a hurry to return to his other patients, he might have noted that Cornelius hadn't answered. Now Cornelius stood by the head of the bed looking down at the sleeping baby and all he said was "Hmmmph" and left.

Lena woke the infant for nursing.

But Olga had noted the odd reaction of Cornelius to his newborn son, and she was already aware of his disregard for Henry. She also knew Cornelius would be sequestering himself in his private domain upstairs all the nights Lena cared for their child. It was then she knew how she felt about her brother-in-law. She did not like him. Olga was careful to keep her opinion of Cornelius to herself for Lena's sake, but also in fear of being denied the company of her two nephews.

The sound of children in the echoing old house was balm to Lena. And Cornelius was proud of his attractive family; especially on Sunday's when dressed in their best, the neighbors would greet and admire his small sons. The happy, flame-haired Clarence couldn't get enough holding, and Henry, the conversationalist delighted in so many people to talk to. But at home squabbling or messes were a sure guarantee to bring on a scolding. Clarence thrived; Henry was a happy child, and Lena sang and talked to her children as she worked in her home. And carrying the youngest on one hip, she took them with her as she fed and watered the chickens, letting Henry toss feed to them.

Cleaning the henhouse took coordination with Belle who came, with Maren, for time with the two boys she so doted on. Lena would deal with all outside work as fast as she could. By one year, Clarence was able to get around and into everything, needing constant eyes protecting him from himself. He crawled faster and walked sooner than Henry had. The fiery-haired boy reminded Lena of Olga as a baby, and she wondered if he was going to take after her energetic sister.

A cot in the music room had become permanent for the visits from Olga, but in her absence, Henry was sleeping in it until a bed of his own could be gotten for him. And the trundle was now Clarence's, also placed in the small room at the insistence of Cornelius.

Lena became a very light sleeper, worried that Clarence would crawl out in the night. It became routine for her to wake and go in to check on her sleeping sons; taking extra care not to wake her sleeping husband.

1904

A TIME TO MOURN AND
A TIME TO DANCE

October had come with all the signs of Fall. Wonderful warm sunny days with cool nights, needing blankets. Fall colors were on the trees and bushes. The garden harvest was over with canning jars now full, and lining shelves in the small stone-lined, dirt-floored cellar located under the winter kitchen, and accessed through the pantry. Lena would quietly check on the boys in the night to re-cover them. They couldn't seem to keep from losing their blankets as they turned in their sleep. It seemed to her they were almost as active in sleep as they were awake. Tonight she lingered; tired, unhappy--and angry. She was pregnant, again, and not feeling well. Cornelius had known for several months, and remained in a black mood, as if it was all her fault--or could it be he really did not know how pregnancies happened? Ha! This one would be here early January. What an awful time to have a baby! "If only it's a girl" was the recurring hope, "perhaps Cornelius would be happier. He'd said, 'better be a girl', as if she had any say in the matter."

Cornelius would need to check out the living room stove and chimney, as well as fill the small coal room with the winter supply of coal. The split wood was already neatly stacked in the woodshed. A mouse had skittered out as she gathered an armful a day or so ago. She would need to remind Cornelius that a cat was needed to keep down rodents. He hated cats, and there were none that she knew of on their property; but an infestation of mice was worse than a cat or two by far. But bringing up anything he didn't want to hear kept a black cloud over Lena's mind until it finally had to be dealt with. She wondered what made him so hard to live with.

Cornelius had cleaned the stove and chimney and filled the belly of the stove, ready now, as the temperatures were already steadily dropping. The coal bucket he set still half full by the stove.

Lena moved between cook stove and table putting the family meal together as she kept an eye on her small sons as they played with spoons and lids, laughing and noisy. She was about seven months along now, awkward and uncomfortable. She could hear Cornelius come in and she set the tea kettle of warm water on the reservoir for him to take with him to the bedroom to wash up. The summer kitchen was now too cold to wash in and the door had to be kept closed till spring. Coming into the warm kitchen, he picked up the kettle and continued on to the bedroom without speaking, and Lena continued with her cooking. Henry watched, following her from stove to pantry and back again. She hadn't seen Clarence follow his father to the living room. When she heard the angry voice of Cornelius and the cry of Clarence at the same time, she threw down the vegetable pan and potholder in a clatter on the table and rushed into the living room to see Cornelius gripping a coal-covered Clarence by his body, holding him away from himself. The baby had found the bucket with coal and in tasting it, smeared black drool across his face, dripped it on his shirt front and had very black hands. Cornelius was angry, and he shoved the now screaming child at his mother and told her, "Clean him up!" He then scooped up the coal from the floor and put the bucket in the coal room. Lena tried to comfort the boy. Little by little the cries decreased, but he still sobbed, and moved his legs as though he hurt somewhere, but as much as she checked him over, he seemed unhurt. Wiping his tears, and murmuring to him, she came back to the kitchen and soon had her family around the table, saying grace, with sobby whimpers still coming from Clarence. She kept him on her lap as she coaxed him to eat. He was always a hearty eater but now, though he tried, he would turn his head away and lean into his mother. She wondered what Cornelius had done. Or had Clarence swallowed a piece of coal? That night she rocked him to sleep in the heavy oak rocker. He was exhausted but seemed restless and needed to feel her nearness. What a beautiful little boy, with Aunt Olga's wild hair. It was late when she put him in his trundle bed and, tired as she was, she got up in the night to check on him. At least he wasn't restless now.

But in the morning Clarence was a fussy little boy, not at all his usual self. Lena carried him much of the time, or he cried, and as she prepared the boys for bed that night, she thought he felt warmer than usual. She whispered a little prayer that was a "Please don't let him be coming down with anything." Carrying him so much that day had left her with a more painful back. By morning she didn't feel much better, and neither did Clarence. His cheeks were flushed and his eyes looked dull. He dropped his head on her shoulder as she lifted him from his bed.

Again he refused food, but after searching she found a bottle with a nipple and holding him, did coax him into sucking water. Dipping a washcloth in cold water she cooled his forehead, trying to bring down the temperature of a now lethargic little boy. By afternoon Lena sent Cornelius for the doctor. And a subdued Henry stood by looking at his mother's anxious face. He didn't understand what was wrong, but he knew something was very wrong.

The over-worked doctor dropped everything and in his own horse buggy followed Cornelius home. Pulling a chair up beside Lena in the rocker, with her sick son across her lap, he was a reassuring presence, but he had no answer for what might be wrong. Lena told him of the coal, wondering if swallowing a piece could cause this. Other than listening to Clarence's lungs, and taking his temperature, Doc Murdock could only surmise the child was coming down with something, but no rash or red areas had yet appeared. Lena could only continue as she had been doing--push water and give cold compresses.

Cornelius had gone for Belle who arrived without Maren this time, and in her calm, efficient way took over as Lena cared for her son. Belle had brought a little gift for the two little boys. It was to have been an Easter gift, a ball in soft Easter colors but decided an early gift was in order. Lena picked up the ball and as Clarence lay across her lap, his head in the crook of her arm, she held the pretty Easter ball close to his dreamy eyes, coaxing him, and placed it in his open hand and he curled his fingers on his new toy, and gazing dreamily at it, he simply slipped away. The ball fell from his hand, bounced on the floor, then rolling slower and slower it stopped.

Clarence Bernhard Erickson, 18 months old, died October 22nd, 1904. The doctor's death report stated the child died of ruptured appendix.

Lena took to her bed. Belle stayed and took over the house. Ole brought Karen and Olga, and while Karen took Henry under her wing, Olga crawled on to Lena's bed, wrapped her arms around her, and both cried until there were no more tears.

Cots appeared from somewhere and were made up for family that stayed. Cornelius seemed at a loss to know what to say or do. Hans and Ole helped with the animals. The minister and undertaker arranged the funeral. The trundle bed had been carried upstairs by someone, but no one ever really knew who. Henry didn't want to go to bed at night without Clarence; and he began to be inconsolable at bedtime. Olga placed her cot next to his, and with her arm over him, he slept.

Olga stayed after everyone left. She and Karen quietly talked of things that troubled them. They believed the marriage was not good, but Lena's thinness and disinterest in anything worried them most. And right now, Henry really needed someone. Both women thought Cornelius incapable of looking after the needs of his wife and son. Also he could not leave his livestock untended, but Hans and Ole also needed to return to their own responsibilities. Olga knew she had the freedom to help her sister until the new baby arrived. And, longer if needed. And stay she did, grieving with and for her sister--pushing her to get up, to eat the good meals Olga set before her. It was a slow process, taking just one day at a time. Henry was only two-and-a-half and needed his mother in this traumatic time.

By December winter had set in with a vengeance and the big house was drafty as it caught the full force of the howling wind. Snow could be found on the windowsills of the north side upstairs windows. Cornelius tacked weather stripping around door jambs and nailed a tough opaque covering over the screen doors. Most of the windows had storm windows, but not the odd size half windows beneath sloped ceilings on the second floor. The first winter in the house Cornelius carried the heavy storm windows up the high ladder to the second level with great difficulty. And there they stayed till the house was torn down many years later.

Together, Lena and Olga resumed household routines and put on an appearance of normalcy as much as possible for the sake of Henry. Olga would soon dress Henry for bed, so Lena warmed her flat irons in the oven, to be wrapped in flannel and tucked into bed with Henry. Somehow, they would get through this bitter time. She held her hands out over the heat of the stove and hated how chapped and rough they were and always cold. "Please God, let Olga stay to help me. Please," was her constant prayer. Olga would be 21 on June 22nd and Lena knew her sister was chafing to be away, anywhere, doing something worthwhile. She knew when the girl turned 21, there would be no stopping her.

Olga was in correspondence with people she knew through her own friends and acquaintances who had gone to bigger cities, who encouraged her in her aspirations. She, like Cornelius, kept abreast of current events, and politics from the newspapers. Olga's opinions differed drastically from his, and they aggravated him in no small way. Women's rights always came up with Olga, and as much as she admired President Roosevelt, she was impatient over his foot-dragging in that arena.

In Cornelius' mind, Olga needed to learn her proper place, and the sooner the better. He did not like her influence on Lena. He hoped she would marry soon and be brought under control by a husband.

Lena wondered if at times her sister was deliberately saying things to get under his skin. And in that moment, she knew without a doubt, that was exactly what that impish girl was doing. Lena tried to smother the laugh that started by putting her hand over her mouth and it came out as a snort. And then the tears burned behind her eyelids again. "Clarence. Clarence. Clarence."

Christmas passed unnoticed except for a fruitcake Olga had craved--and then baked. Near Christmas Lena mentioned she hadn't had lefse since she was married which put Olga on the mission of making up a batch like their mother had frequently made. The peeling and boiling of potatoes began, milk was heated and flour seemed to go everywhere. A lefse "kjevle" was borrowed from the couple living in a small house at the base of the Erickson hill. Henry was fascinated; drawn by the happy camaraderie of the sisters, as well as all the flour on the floor. It was a pleasant time much needed by all three. And the lefse wasn't too bad for two novices. Even Cornelius was pleased.

But it was on that trip to the neighbors to borrow the kjevle that Lena learned the couple were renters of the property from Cornelius. He'd never told her it was part of the farm--used at one time to house the hired hand and his family. Any, and all deeds or important business papers by-passed her and went into Cornelius' locked desk-box, with no explanations. Deepening resentment and anger towards him smoldered.

Before the new year arrived, Cornelius had hitched up one of the horses to the carriage and made repeated trips up and down the hill until he was sure the doctor could reach them when Lena's time came. Cornelius was absolutely sure of one thing: he wanted nothing to do with birthing. So, for any amount of snowfall from then on, he drove the horse and carriage up and down the hill.

Between Lena and Olga a layette was again ready and waiting for the next arrival. Lena refused to dwell on the sex of the child. It was less stressing to just not think about it. In her mirror over the dressing table, she could see how shapeless and bulky she was, and her hairbrush revealed the increase of hair loss. She noted her hair looked duller and drier. It was bad enough to see these unwelcome changes, but to know her husband found her disgusting was something else. The only positive thing she could find in her situation was,--he stayed away from her.

The third of January dawned mild, sunny, melting some of the snow. Which most likely was the reason Hans, Maren and Belle came jingling up the hill mid-morning looking forward to a good visit, and time with Henry. Olga was busy with the butter churn, and Lena was making up stories for Henry as they sat in the rocking chair by the coal stove. Seeing Belle's entrance excited Henry as much as Olga's arrivals always had. He was blessed to have two such special aunts. Belle had brought cold chicken and dried raisins, as well as molasses cookies. Olga set out chunks of cheese and pickles, then sliced fresh bread and used the just churned butter to make chicken sandwiches. It was coffee with cream and sugar for the grown-ups, and milk for Henry, and Olga, who liked fresh cold milk as much as her nephew. The voices mixed pleasantly around the table, and tidbits of news were exchanged. Time goes too fast in pleasant hours. In a rare pause, Maren spoke, reminding Belle of the postcard in her handbag, which sent Belle hustling to the bedroom where the bag had been left with the coats. Herman, the youngest of Cornelius' family, had sent his parents the postcard to be shared with family and friends. It was dated December 10th, but the news was he and Hilda had a baby girl born November 15th, and her name was Doris. Her two older brothers were delighted with her.

Maren and Belle were pleased to share Herman and Hilda's happiness, not realizing behind Cornelius' pleasantly nodding head, resentment seethed. No one could have wanted a girl more than he. Lena gave the same pleasant response, saying, "How wonderful for them," while in the dark corners of her mind, she knew this news would not go well with Cornelius. Lena hadn't shared with anyone the times Cornelius had spoken of his preference for a daughter.

The men picked up their chairs and retreated to the living room for farmer talk around the pot belly stove. Cornelius returned to pick up his coffee cup for a refill, and looking at Belle, he held it up with a smiling "thank you" nod. She had brought him his own cup from when he'd lived at home. It was a mustache cup. And he was genuinely pleased.

Lena despised it from the moment she saw it.

There was very little to clear away before the four women could get back to the visiting they so enjoyed. Belle and Olga dragged the heavy rocker to the kitchen for Lena where she sank into it and held out her hands to a sleepy Henry. Once on her lap, his head in the crook of her arm, close to the warm stove, he was asleep so fast that Belle had to laugh. Maren and Belle sat on the two remaining chairs, and Olga perched herself on the kindling box and leaned on the wall. It was a very good day for Lena, and she slept peacefully that night without nightmares.

The following day she talked to Olga about the new art-craft that Belle was so excited over. Imagine using human hair to create bouquets of flowers! Lena could not envision it, but Belle was adamant as she had not only seen a framed display, she and the church ladies were meeting in each others' homes and cutting long strands of each others' hair and were twisting, coiling and rolling it into petals and stems. The various colors were amazing. That was certainly something to think about.

Three days passed before the low backache alerted Lena that her labor had begun. The contractions were mild most of the day, but by evening had intensified. Cornelius made the trip to Dr. Murdock in the afternoon and the doctor had checked on Lena after he closed his office. With a sigh, he predicted the baby would most likely arrive pre-dawn. Thinking things through, he told the anxious family he would return around 10 pm--unless they sent for him sooner. So he went to his supper, and to let his wife know he would be with the Ericksons for the night. Cornelius lay down fully dressed on his bed at 9 pm. Olga lay down fully dressed beside Lena. When the doctor came back, he stretched out on Olga's empty cot at ten-thirty. It had been moved to the living room to keep from waking Henry.

Olga wiped perspiration from Lena's face through the night and gave her sips of water. Close to 4 am, Olga knew something had changed when she heard the soft moans through clenched teeth and rushed to wake the doctor. By 4:15 the doctor was clamping and cutting the cord of a loudly crying--boy! Cornelius had been called, and was waiting in the living room, while Olga cleaned up and wrapped a healthy baby who appeared bald at first glance but on close examination had strawberry blonde fuzz that would change over time to the light brown of the uncle he would never meet—Lena's brother, Hendriek. His eyes would be a warm brown. Cornelius as usual looked once at his son and said nothing. He saw the doctor off, then dressed in work clothes and went out in the dark to feed livestock. Lena held the infant close, protectively. In an hour he was nursing, while Olga hovered over mother and baby. Quietly, she asked, "Have you a name for him?" And Lena nodded, but didn't speak for several minutes. Then, without taking her eyes from her new son she said, "His name is Clarence Bernhard."

Olga was speechless. Fear for Lena's rationality raced through her. Had everything become too much for her to cope with? "Why, Lena? Why? Is this a good thing?"

Lena, looking up, saw the fear on her sister's face, and felt remorse. But she was set upon the name and was not to be talked out of it. "Why? Because I want Clarence remembered every time they hear or say his name. And I especially want Cornelius to never forget."

Hearing those words, a burden lifted for Olga who feared her quiet, work-worn sister wasn't strong enough emotionally to not break under the cold, controlling Cornelius and the loss of her precious child. It was all so much. Lena's daily existence wasn't easy. But on hearing those words, Olga knew there was a strength in Lena that would carry her through. And that was good to know, as Olga knew she would have to be leaving one of these days, before Henry became too attached. Or before Cornelius asked her to go. She knew she was an irritant to him, for which she felt a little guilt. Just a small amount, though, as he was just as much an irritant to her.

She stayed long enough to celebrate Clarence's baptism; helping to put him in the gown his two older brothers had been baptized in. He was a plumper baby than they had been. And also, he was an easy baby, not fussy, a good sleeper. February was half gone when Olga began preparations to return home to her parents. Lena had known this day would come when she would have to let her go. Olga had her own life to live. As the suitcase was being packed, Lena felt like crying, and struggled against it. "What will I do without you, Sis?! I hate to see you leave, but I understand--I do!" And Olga, taking both her sister's hands in her own, answered, "You are so much stronger than you even know, Lena. Don't forget that. Ever." They said their goodbyes with Cornelius waiting in the carriage to take Olga to the bus station. She tried not to look back at the thin, forlorn figure standing on the east porch as they passed, but then she did, and raised a hand in farewell.

Henry and the baby filled Lena's days, as well as parts of the nights nursing Clarence. She kept the thoughts of Olga and how much she missed her entertaining sister at bay. It was peaceful in the living room with the lamp turned low, sitting by the warm stove, rocking as she nursed Clarence, humming all the nursery songs she knew. She kept the baby's cradle close enough to the coal stove for warmth, and far enough away for safety. When he was hungry in the night, she could hear the smacking-sucking sounds on his fists first, soon followed by tiny vocal grunts, increasing in volume until she picked him up. Lena was grateful Cornelius was upstairs in his own room. She didn't care if he never slept in her bed again. In the quietness of the night Lena thought her way through the coming day: what would be the priorities to be dealt with first, and on down the mental "to-do" list. It helped to feel organized, and to avoid chaos, which could happen in the blink of an eye.

Cornelius had taken her suggestion of having a cat to keep the rodent population down, and in April had come home with a young female cat in a bag. Females were good hunters, males were not. Now it was Lena's job to tame and entice the cat to stay. She had been giving it saucers of creamy milk in the woodshed and even named the cat "Mitzie". It now came out of hiding when Lena entered with the milk. It was a short-hair, buff colored with white paws and chest, and Lena hoped it would solve any mouse problems. Hopefully, once it was let out, it would return for milk at the back door.

When the weather was cold Lena churned the butter in the house, but as it warmed she longed to be outside in fresh air and sunshine, taking Henry with her so he could run and play. She placed Clarence on a blanket, just inside the screen door where she kept an eye on him as she churned the butter. Months earlier she had asked Cornelius to make a workbench for her at the back door where she sat on the cement cleaning vegetables and shelling peas, but he hadn't done so. Now she carried a kitchen chair out to sit on as she worked and watched her children. Cornelius had business in town, and would have his lunch at the restaurant, no doubt, so coming in from the butter-making, Lena fixed Henry's lunch, and sat in the rocker nursing Clarence before putting both boys down for a nap. The sun had disappeared, and the sky darkened. The sound of rain came, spattering the windows on the south and west where no porches offered protection. With the boys napping, Lena set about planning the evening meal, checking what she had, and what needed to be used up. The salt pork needed to be used: checking on how many potatoes were in the basket, she decided "komel" was the meal choice for the day.

Putting extra wood in the stove and opening the damper, Lena put her flat irons on the stove in preparation for ironing yesterday's laundry. She had paused finally in the ironing to push the coffee pot, with leftover coffee, on to warm, and took a much-needed rest for her aching back and tired shoulders. The rain had stopped and her thoughts went to the gardening that would soon be the next priority; planting time was coming up fast. Setting her cup in the pantry with the lunch dishes, to be washed up after the evening meal, she picked up the folded clothes for putting away in the bedrooms. Carrying the folded shirts up the stairs to Cornelius' room, her eyes wandered over each open doorway into the empty bedrooms. Cornelius' room was the only one with anything in it—three-quarter sized bed which she noted he had pulled the blankets smoothly into place. She could smell the strong odor of tobacco and saw the pipe resting on a glass plate with a tin of tobacco next to it. It was an unpleasant odor to Lena. But the room was neat and orderly with a low dresser under a mirror. She placed the folded shirts in the bottom drawer. The old sailor's desk sat on top of the dresser, and she idly reached out a hand, and with a finger, tried to lift up on the lid. Locked, as usual. She wondered why he was so secretive about his precious box. She knew the property deed was in there--but why would he think she couldn't be trusted? She had never given him a reason to distrust her. But she did wonder about him since learning of the renters.

Lately, she had begun thinking of talking to him about allowing her to have the egg money for household expenses. On returning to the kitchen, she found Cornelius standing there with a water-stained kitchen chair in front of him. He was not pleased. Hurriedly, she rubbed it with rags, explaining how it had come to be forgotten--and silently hoping it had no lasting damage. Time would tell. But now was not the time to bring up the egg money. And that was the day Cornelius began putting together a bench for Lena.

Lena's Workbench and Corn Planter

The planting of the garden was essential, a necessity. The turning and smoothing of the soil had been done, and now Lena placed seeds in neat rows, leaving markers identifying what would be growing. Henry played within sight, and Clarence fussed on a blanket on the grass. He didn't like not being picked up when he could see his mother near, but busy with something besides himself.

With the boys fed and down for their naps Lena was finishing the garden work, glad to see the job done.

1905

A TIME TO CAST AWAY STONES AND A TIME TO GATHER STONES TOGETHER

The seeds had sprouted in the neat rows, watched over by Lena as she and Henry checked on the young plants daily. It was where they were when Hans and Belle made a rapid entrance up the hill, circling the house and pulling the sweating horse to an abrupt stop, bits of foamy saliva flecked its muzzle. Hans sat for a moment as Belle jumped to the ground. Alarm ran through Lena as she ran to them. Something bad has happened! Belle was so serious but in a calm voice she said, "Father needs to talk to you, Lena." I will look after Henry and the baby." Then smiling for Henry, she led him into the house. Hans had gotten down from the buggy, and taking Lena's arm, asked her to "come, sit down," and led her to the bench Cornelius had finished putting together for her. Cornelius was out in his fields working. She had begun to feel lightheaded, with a terrible foreboding, and wanted to be anywhere else than here in this moment. Hans seated her on the bench; and then took what seemed like a long time to say what he had come so quickly to say. "I'm sorry, Lena--so sorry. Ole called us to tell you to please come. Quickly. It is your sister--Olga. She is very sick."

Lena heard her own voice coming from a distance, sounding odd. "Why? What has happened?" and she learned Olga was sick from drinking unpasteurized milk. The cows were infected with brucellosis. The brook water was contaminated. Now, as Hans urged her to get ready and go, she resisted, saying, "But surely she will be all right! Won't she? She's strong, and healthy."

But Hans shook his head sadly and told her, "They hoped so, but the doctor now says she will not survive. Go. Get ready. I will go to your neighbor, Stener. If he cannot drive you there, he will know someone who can."

She felt as though she were walking in a dream. Nothing seemed real. But she did as Hans told her, and once in the house, Belle calmly, and capably talked her through her preparation, reassuring her all the while that her boys were in good hands: that a baby formula was now in the drug store, and Clarence would be fine. Hans returned to say the Thorsons would be coming for her in thirty minutes. Stener's wife, Gertrude, had wanted to accompany her. In the meantime, Hans was going to wait for Cornelius to come in from the field.

Soon, still feeling disembodied, she was in the Thorsons motor car, her first time to ride in one and she felt caught up in a nightmare, unable to wake up. Months would pass before she would recall she never thanked them. They had been so kind, allowing her the silence she needed.

Home. It still looked, felt like home, and she wished she were a child again where mother and father could make everything right again. She walked into an empty kitchen, then on through the front room to the stairs leading to their old bedrooms. She ascended almost soundlessly; it was Olga who always clattered up and down those steps. Then she was at the open doorway to Olga's silent room. The doctor sat in a chair at the head of the bed, her parents had pulled the flat-top trunk to the other side, and there they huddled together, haggard and looking old beyond their years. She forced herself to look at the still form in the single bed. A form much diminished since she'd last seen her sister. Now there were dark circles beneath the sunken eyes, cheek bones prominent beneath the white, dry skin. Was she even breathing? Conscious? Olga was near death; the terrible pain and nausea was over. Seeing her, the doctor stood and motioned her to the chair. Sinking weakly into the proffered seat, Lena reached out and lifted the limp cold hand, holding it between both her own, wanting to warm it, but her own were almost as cold. Instead she bowed her head over her sister's hand and kissed it. There were the muffled sounds of Maren's weeping, and a shuffle as Ole slowly rose and left the room, to be quickly followed by Maren pressing a hanky over most of her face.

Lena stroked the cold hand and raised her eyes to find Olga's eyes had opened and were looking back at her. How sick they looked. Where had all that sparkling spirit gone? She was struggling to say something, but her colorless lips failed. Lena leaned close, putting her ear to the moving mouth. Olga whispered something. And looking again into Olga's eyes, Lena said, "I will. I promise." A quietness came over Olga's face, and the tired eyes closed.

Olga Erickson, Lena's Sister

The doctor wondered what it was his dying patient had whispered to her sister, but thought it was not for him to pry.

By evening on May 11th Olga died taking with her the joyful laughter that could set others laughing.

Her burial was in the Highland Prairie Church yard, near where Hendriek lay. When the minister spoke the words of "ashes to ashes, and dust to dust," with the sound of handfuls of soil hitting the coffin, the finality of it all was heartbreaking.

Before summer was over, a stone with name and dates, marked her grave.

Lena had stayed with her parents until after the funeral, but then returned with Cornelius who had come for the interment. Now it was necessary she be home with her boys. Hidden in her travel bag, Lena carried home with her a lock of Olga's hair, acquired with help from the undertaker.

Belle's sharp eyes took in Lena's weariness, wondering how this sister-in-law she cared so much for was holding up under such crushing losses, one following another in such a short time. And, much as she loved her brother, she was not blind to the fact he was not an easy person to live with. She had puzzled more than once over how he had managed to catch the lovely Lena and, why, when even Belle could see no great passion for him in Lena. Now, though, her concern was for Lena and the two precious boys. Maren had been doing the best she could on her own while Lena was gone, and Belle was determined to stay as long as she felt needed, but she knew her mother needed her, too. As she watched Lena, she was grateful to see her holding up as well as she was. Perhaps she was stronger than Belle thought. Yes, Belle would soon need to be on her way home to Maren. Besides, Lena knew she had only to send for her, and she would be right back. Belle hoped Cornelius would install a telephone, now that he knew how convenient it was to have one.

Lena gave thanks for the generous heart and hands of Belle--what a blessing this woman was. As happy as Henry had been to see his mother again, he still wanted Belle to stay, and was quite determined about it, which pleased his aunt greatly.

In order to keep nursing Clarence, Lena had had to resort to a breast pump. Now the old order of her routine quickly resumed, and she leaned heavily on her sister's urgent last request. Olga had used the last of her own strength to instill in Lena the strength and fortitude she herself had, and that she knew her sister to be weaker in. She would need endurance in the life she'd lead with Cornelius. She had only herself now.

Summer had two sides for Lena. She had to be outside much of the time with gardening, the laundry, and clean for the chickens--all hard work. Anything indoors got much less attention. But her sons thrived in the outdoors, finding their playthings in nature. They were so joyful and exuberant. Her eyes, as well as Clarence's followed Henry's every move. It was obvious that as soon as he crawled, he'd be following his busy brother everywhere.

She always left cleaning the coop to the time the boys napped. This day, working rapidly, she made up her mind to push Cornelius to turn the egg money over to her for household things as well as clothes for Henry who was growing so fast. She found it demeaning asking for money for every little thing. He always had to think her requests through, often stating one thing or another was unnecessary. Or too expensive. Then he'd put them on hold for awhile, before grudgingly giving her an amount just under what she'd requested. This time there would be no backing down. Hurrying into the house, she just had time to wash the filth off and change her clothes before hearing Henry trotting out of his room, after waking Clarence up.

When the boys were in bed for the night; and dishes and kitchen work done, Lena came from the pantry carrying an empty fruit jar with a zinc lid. Pausing for just a moment to take a deep breath, and assess Cornelius reading his paper (again) close to the lamp on the kitchen table, while smoking his pipe, she advanced slowly enough to get his attention. Looking up at her with a puzzled frown starting across his brow, he set his pipe down in its rest.

Coming to the table, maintaining a steady, but calm, eye contact, Lena set the jar in front of him with just a little smack. Clearly, but pleasantly, Lena spoke, going straight to the point. "This jar is for the egg money that I need, want, expect, and am entitled to. Should this not happen, you will need to hire someone to clean for the chickens, feed them, and collect eggs daily." And with that said, she picked up her mending basket and sitting across from him, pulled out a sock to darn, shoving a wooden egg down to a large hole in the heel, and reached for the darning thread: waiting.

And it came--barely controlled, self-righteous anger. "You think there is so much money, you can just demand? And for what nonsense would you need it? No!"

Raising her eyes to his, still in a calm voice, she gave a nod first at the pipe and tobacco, then towards the paper. "You find money enough for all that nonsense and for your occasional lunch out." Then removing the darning egg from the sock with a hole in the heel, she casually tossed his sock in his direction and it landed over his pipe. Then said, "Use some of your precious money to buy yourself new socks next time you take yourself out for lunch." Tossing the scissor, thread, and egg into their basket, she picked it up and took herself off to bed. She hoped he'd come around. She doubted he would. The shakiness in her knees had subsided, and as she entered her dressing room, she tilted her head back, eyes closed, and whispered, "I did it, Olga! I did it!" And for the first time in a very long time, she was happy. A stone was lifted.

The minutes ticked by, and Cornelius felt in a turmoil. He was angry; wondering what had set her off. He knew he intimidated her, that she wanted peace above all, and refused to fight, so it had never bothered him to exert control over her. He liked things that way. It must have something to do with losing her sister. Olga always had too much influence over her. He was actually not sorry Olga was out of their life. This was probably not a good time to put Lena in her place. Fine! Let her have her damn egg money. It wasn't that much anyway.

This was no small victory for Lena. She felt lighter in spirit, more sure of herself. No more begging for the things the young family needed, used, or just enjoyed. She even bought herself a jar of hand cream for her roughened hands, and felt no guilt at all, and a wooden train for Henry, and a small soft bear for Clarence.

She learned to hitch one of the horses to the carriage; and Cornelius was powerless to prevent her. She began to make time for herself, attending a quilting group of women who met once a month. Handling the colorful fabric was like balm to her. She joined a Bible Study group who met before church, and the boys played in the nursery with other children, and they were delighted with their new playmates.

Occasionally, Lena's sister-in-law Carrie and her husband Chris would come with their son, Hildus, to visit. Hildus was the same age as Clarence and the women had much in common, and always so much to catch up on. Carrie was a lot like Belle, outgoing and fun. They talked of the photography business that had recently opened in Mabel and made future plans to photograph their children when they were older. Carrie said Chris talked of wanting a motor car, and Lena stated Cornelius had no use for them, a waste of money in his opinion. He held the same attitude for the telephone contraption since it was something he had no intention of using and therefore Lena didn't need one either.

Postcards with the 1-cent postage kept Lena in touch with her parents after Olga died, though the distance between them was a matter of only a few miles. Lena's children were her priority; she had no phone, and no way to have frequent contact. Cornelius had the farm to run; and the busiest time of year for farmers was in full force.

Karen was brief in her cards due to limited space, and no wish to air her concerns to all the public. But also, she did not want to add to Lena's burdens.

The day Lena stood beside Olga's bedside, her parents had seen how tired, thin, and unhappy she was, and they regretted from the depths of already breaking hearts, their part in pushing Lena into a marriage that never should have happened.

Their remorse, coupled with the loss of Olga, was overwhelming. Ole had no choice but to work, and keep the farm running smoothly. It was their livelihood. For Karen, it seemed her life had lost all meaning; and her interest in anything that had been meaningful to her faded into nothingness. Gradually her postcards stopped.

Ole watched and worried. Nothing he could say changed anything. Even threatening to send for Lena had no effect other than to cause a storm of tears, and words to the effect that they had already caused too much harm to Lena. So he said nothing.

The summer months passed; the harvest came and was very good everywhere. But when the brilliant colors of fall came, and Karen seldom got up from her bed--and then only with help, Ole knew Lena had to be told. Ole had installed a telephone hoping to interest Karen to reach out to friends, but it didn't work. Now Ole used it to call Hans and Maren. He needed them once again to go to Lena and Cornelius with the report of Karen's failing health.

Hans made the trip to his son's farm alone, timing it to arrive late when Cornelius would be in for the night. It meant a return by lantern, but the horse knew the way home and would be eager to be back into its stall for food and water.

Hans wondered if Lena and Cornelius had seen him pass the kitchen windows as he circled around the large grounds the house sat on, and then pulled up just short of the woodshed. By the time he reached the first kitchen entrance Cornelius was holding the screen door open. Though his son greeted him warmly, Hans was sure he and Lena had to be wondering what bad news was being delivered this late in the day. Invited to "Come on in," Hans followed, and once in the main kitchen saw Lena, holding Clarence. Henry still sat at the supper table, finishing his meal. Apologizing for interrupting them, Hans insisted they finish eating, saying they could talk over coffee. It was obvious the meal was strained, but it was gotten through without upsetting the boys. Henry was allowed a little play time before dressing for bed. Hans opened his arms for hugs before the boy ran off. Lena stayed seated with Clarence on her lap, her eyes never leaving Hans' face. She seemed to know the news involved her.

The color was fading from her face, but her voice was clear, steady; "Who is it this time?" was all she said.

"Your father called, asking I let you know your mother is not well. She seems to have lost the will to live, Lena. The doctor can find nothing wrong. Ole thinks you need to come." He delivered the unwelcome news in short, jerky sentences, and wished someone, anyone else could have delivered the news. Looking at his frozen-faced daughter-in-law, all he could think was, "This poor woman!"

Before Hans began his return home, the three of them had their plans set: Hans was sure Belle would again look after the boys; and whether or not Maren came along or stayed home would be up to her. And by going by bus it would be faster than if Cornelius took her there by horse and carriage. The day after tomorrow was when she would leave.

With party line telephones, and local switch board operators, the news spread like grassfire. Before noon the next day, Stener Thorson was standing on the Ericksons' east porch, offering to drive Lena to her parents' farm again. And Lena, with tears, humbly thanked him for his offer, along with a belated thanks for the first time, too. Gertrude wanted to ride along again if Lena didn't mind.

Once again, she was on her way to her old home, but this time she and Gertrude visited for some of the time. A friendship had developed between the two women in their time together in the quilting group, though, "Gertie" was a few years older. The older woman questioned Lena if she planned to butcher and preserve the older hens when they quit laying, and if she planned to fill feather pillows with the down. It hadn't occurred to Lena, but now her interest was piqued, and she plied her friend for directions on the whole process. And laughing, the pleasant Gertie offered to help her through the whole messy process. Leaning back on the hard leather seat, Lena thought, "It's good not feeling alone."

Home didn't really feel like home this time. There was an abandoned atmosphere throughout the house. It was dusty, with evidence of neglect everywhere. The beating heart of this home had been her mother. Why had it stopped? Why did she give up? But Lena knew that she, herself, had wanted to give up. Everything just hurt so much—so many painful changes. She recognized that she and her mother shared a weakness. The fighter, the scrappy one is--had been--Olga. And Olga had seen this in Lena, and fought for her, to her last breath. But the strong one was gone. Lena was in a fight for herself every day, for her sons' sakes. What did she have left to help her mother?!

Everything seemed out of place now in Karen's formerly pristine home. Sitting beside her mother's bed, Lena talked to her in a low voice, holding her hand, sometimes stroking it, sometimes patting. She offered chicken broth, begging her to swallow just a spoonful, but the mouth stayed closed.

When Lena had arrived Lena touched her and called her "Mother". Karen had heard, and opening her eyes, looking at Lena with such sorrow, whispered, "I'm sorry." Then closing her eyes, drifted back to sleep, shutting everything, and everyone out. She lingered two more days. Karen Johana Olson Hogenson died October 30, 1905; her grave was next to Olga's.

Ole farmed but didn't socialize. The hired man, being local came and went as needed, and was on his own for meals. Ole managed with the bare minimum for his meals--whatever was simple or easy. He used only two rooms in the house--kitchen and bedroom, while dust settled more thickly over everything. He hired a woman in town to do his laundry and, for awhile, continued to attend church services, until he deemed his clothes too shabby to be seen there. He supported the church as usual, but he didn't buy clothes unless he had no choice. He disliked shopping.

Lena came twice to see him and left depressed at the state of her childhood home. Ole was glad seeing her, but the conversation was slow and strained. She urged her father to take time for himself--to come for visits with his grandsons and her. He would agree, pleasantly enough, but never followed through. Eventually, he sold all the livestock and worked only crop land. Ole became a recluse.

Lena kept her mind as busy as she could to keep from dwelling on the losses and changes in her family. She couldn't change anything, so when sadness came--and it did--she would look for the good things in life, counting them over in her mind the way a miser might count gold. She had her boys. She had Belle, and Maren, Hans, and Carrie--her new family--and she knew they cared about her. She had close friends in her church. She had her delightful quilting group, and good neighbors. Her core strength was her faith.

1905 with all its losses and pain passed as promised, "This, too, shall pass": winter, spring, summer. Cornelius at last had a hired hand helping on the busy farm. Lena ran her household efficiently, as well as caring for garden and chickens. And Cornelius tossed the egg money on the table regularly, with no comment.

1906 came and went. Sunday was the day of rest, as much as possible, after animal care. Sunday mornings found the family dressed and ready early to attend Lena's Bible Study while Cornelius attended to needs of the church property.

But this particular perfect summer day as members said their good-byes and departed, Henry fell down the cement steps leading to the great double doors. Lena and Cornelius didn't see it happen, but hearing his screams, rushed to him. One of the elders was picking Henry up as the anxious parents got to him and were told by the elder that Henry was running, tripped and fell down the steps. It was obvious there was going to be a lump on his head above an eye, and there was a bleeding cut across the left knee cap. Henry cried all the way home, and Cornelius scolded him for running on the steps telling him he was too big to cry.

Lena's lips tightened, wanting to silence Cornelius. Five-to-six-year-old boys ran. They fell. And they sometimes hurt themselves and cried. This was normal. Once home, Lena cleaned the cut, decided no stitches were needed, and dressed Henry's knee with a wrapping of gauze.

1907--Henry turned six that September, and would be attending school, something he was very excited about. His best friend in church school would be in his class and seeing Eli every day was just simply the best thing ever.

Lena had other things on her mind besides readying Henry for school. She knew there would be another addition to the family, sometime early in April, and all the old familiar dread of facing Cornelius came crashing in again. The noise, mess, disorder that came with babies and children he simply did not like and did not adapt well to. So this time she didn't tell him. It would only be a matter of time and the evidence would be impossible to miss. She at times wondered what the preacher would say if she asked him, "If the punishment meted out in the Garden of Eden fit the crime, then an apple wasn't really the issue. Was it?" And true to form Cornelius' reaction was to blame Lena, the temptress.

She had tried staying up late with mending or sewing clothes for the children only to find herself facing an angry Cornelius in the middle of the night. On occasion she had felt icy fear looking into the black fury of his eyes. When she tried to beg off for fear of pregnancy, he simply brushed her words away. She did nothing to entice him. Lena knew she went out of her way to dress modestly, and kept her hair pulled back in a braided bun. She was no temptress. What ever temptations existed were all in Cornelius' head. There were moments when memories of Lars came uninvited and troubling. Uninvited because looking into a past that couldn't be changed served no purpose but to cause Lena to sink back into the pit of blackness that she'd managed to come through. And troubling, as she could so clearly see now the differences of Lars from Cornelius. The wonderful friendship she knew was there with Lars. His gentleness and kindness. There was something missing in Cornelius that at times gave her a sense of fear she couldn't understand. Lena tried to look neither to the past—or to the future. She had no control of either. Dealing with today was enough.

In October, a postcard from Ole arrived asking Lena if she wanted any furniture from the upstairs bedrooms, or the piano. He had no need of the unused pieces and believed they would find good use in her large home. He would help get them to her if she wanted them. It was a good distraction for Cornelius who was pushing to have the boys sleeping upstairs in hopes of stopping some of Lena's coddling.

For Lena, memories of Olga wanting her to have the piano for the daughter she believed would someday arrive moved her to take it. Henry slept on Olga's cot in the music room. Maybe it was time to make changes.

The three single beds upstairs in Lena's old home, along with the dressers, and washstands were all to be moved, as well as an old corner cupboard that had belonged to Karen's brother, and several trunks. Lena made a last visit to her old home to pack up her mother's

Corner Cupboard Made by Karen's Brother, Lena's Uncle

quilts, tablecloths, china, and silver. So many things her father had just left where Karen had last put them.

A great motorized truck was to carry all the items to their new home. When the driver of the truck arrived at Lena's and Cornelius' home, and stared at the long steep driveway up the hill, he whistled, and shook his head. Neighbors had arrived to help with the unloading once at the top of the hill. But now, at the bottom, extra ropes appeared and were fastened to the piano, and the corner cupboard to keep them upright. The doubtful, nervous driver went at the hill with everything the truck had--roaring, shuddering, shaking--it made it to the top. And the men cheered. Some betting had been going on, and a little cash changed hands. The piano went on a small wagon pulled by horses to the south front porch where it was moved through the doorway with the stained-glass window, into the parlor and from there to the music room. It had made it in one piece.

Henry was asked which of the rooms would he like for his own bed and dresser. After careful consideration of the many choices, he picked the biggest room with the best sunlight, directly over the parlor and facing south. And the farthest from Cornelius room to Lena's relief, in case the boys were noisy enough to disturb their father. Henry then directed where he wanted his bed and dresser. He was quite pleased with everything. There were three connected bedrooms in this area of the upstairs, and the small bedroom was set up with bed and dresser for Clarence, but the trundle that he'd slept in was placed in the walk-through room where he could see into Henry's room and know he wasn't alone. Lena felt comfortable with the arrangement, and Cornelius was pleased with making the boys more independent, as well as with the rooms, filled with good furniture. The corner cupboard went into a corner in Henry's room for storage.

The boys adapted well to their new sleeping arrangements and Lena set about washing the baby clothes and diapers in readiness for the next occupant. Cornelius had been slow to notice the pregnancy, but it wasn't long before he had again installed himself in his own room.

Henry had fallen again on the frozen playground early in January and was still limping two weeks later. Lena had examined the knee, and this time thought it looked a little swollen, and wondered if she should have the doctor look at it. Cornelius looked, and saw nothing out of the ordinary. But Henry continued to limp, and appeared to guard the knee, never kneeling on it, and Lena couldn't get the uneasiness to go away. As her due date came closer, she decided to have the knee examined--easier now she thought, than with a new baby.

As they waited their turn in the doctor's office, the doctor had poked his head out of his exam room to signal his office nurse to come in and seeing them called out a greeting. He also noted how Henry sat with his leg outstretched, a hand on his knee.

As Henry sat on the exam table in his undergarments, the doctor checked him from head to toe. He was weighed, his height measured, Lena was told Henry appeared to be healthy, but was under weight for his age. The recent fall could have aggravated the bad fall last summer. There was definitely some swelling, causing discomfort. Dr. Bruess Liniment was to be rubbed over the joint at bedtime, and a teaspoon of cod liver oil every day was ordered. The doctor would see him again in one week. He had a low-grade fever.

Getting Henry to swallow the cod liver oil after gagging on the first dose became a daily struggle. There was no way to disguise it, and in desperation, Lena turned to Cornelius to do the job.

Over the following week she saw no change in how Henry walked, and no decrease in swelling. A week later, missing a half-day of school, Henry, again in just his undergarments, sat on the exam table. He still had the low-grade fever, and

Lena revealed she thought he was less active now. Carefully, the doctor pressed the flesh around the knee and heard the boy gasp. Asking questions in a casual way of Henry, the doctor began feeling along the ribs, the arm bones, the bones of both legs. "Do you sleep well at night, Henry?" he asked, and the boy replied with a shrug, and a "Sometimes not."

"Why sometimes not, son?" the doctor asked with a smile.

As Lena listened and watched, she knew there was something going on, and she knew the doctor had strong suspicions.

"How about your other leg, Henry; does it ever hurt?"

"Sometimes. Not bad like this one" and Henry put a hand on his left knee.

"Well, Henry, Miriam here is going to help you get dressed; and then she will have a nice treat for you, while I have a talk with your mother."

With a quick nod to the nurse, he ushered Lena to his office. The doctor was more distressed than Lena as he looked at the tired, anxious, near-term woman. He hoped what he had to say wouldn't put her into premature labor. He debated waiting until Cornelius was present, and then chose to move ahead. Lena always seemed more tense when her husband was around. "Lena, I think I know what is going on with Henry. I pray to God I'm wrong. I still need to run a test. Are you able to hear what I have to say? Or do you want to wait till Cornelius is here? Later? So Henry won't be upset? You tell me." And he watched all her emotions pass over her white face.

Then straightening her back and shoulders, Lena looked him in the eye before answering. "Tell me." Just the two terse words from Lena.

Taking a deep breath and placing folded hands on the desk, Dr. Murdock leaned towards Lena and quietly, with as few words as possible, told her he suspected Henry had Ewing's sarcoma. He let her ask the questions, and he answered as clearly as he could: the doctor knew there would be many more questions to be dealt with later.

Lena's face grew ashen—she now knew the basics of the disease and the symptoms to be looking for: constant low-grade fever, leg pain from activity, and also at night. And no, there was no cure.

When Henry's voice could be heard outside the door, the doctor quickly said, "Bring Cornelius here tomorrow. There is much we will need to talk about." Slowly the doctor stood and coming around his desk he took both her hands in his in a gentle squeeze, and then walked her back to Henry who was happily sucking a green sucker.

The rest of the day seemed to pass in a blur, and Lena's hands performed the necessary chores and last meal of the day without engaging her mind. The happy chatter of the two boys was the only sounds she heard. It was their active play her eyes followed. The silent figure seated at the table, pipe in hand, reading the newspaper might as well have been invisible. Lighting another lamp for the living room she set a clothes drying rack near the coal stove and hung all the boys' night wear as near as possible to warm for bedtime. She had the flat irons in the oven again to warm their feet in the cold beds. She was grateful for the feather mattresses on their new beds, and for the plenteous supply of warm blankets. Carrying the heated, wrapped irons in one arm, and the lamp in her right hand, she led her wool-sock-footed sons up the long flight of stairs to their rooms, tucking a warm iron in each bed. Then pointing to the white porcelain pot, pulled out from under Henry's bed, she asked if they needed to "potty" before bed. They did. Then both climbed into Henry's bed. Clarence wanted to sleep with Henry, and since no objection came, Lena retrieved the iron from the trundle and settled them both in a single bed. Seating herself near the foot she smiled at her sons and folded her hands, watching them expectantly, and they each folded their hands and all three closed their eyes and a delicate chorus softly recited "Now I lay me down to sleep. I pray the Lord my soul to keep. If I should die before I wake, I pray the Lord my soul to take." Then she kissed them each good night and walked downstairs with the lamp. Into her bedroom, closing the door, she set the lamp on the dresser. Then picking up her pillow she opened her mouth wide and stuffed as much as she could in, bit down, and screamed.

Cornelius had finished reading his paper and became aware of the quietness around him. Lena must be putting the boys down for the night, and he might as well head for bed, too. Morning would come soon enough with plenty to do readying equipment for spring planting. As he stood up, he heard Lena behind him and was surprised to hear her speaking to him.

"We need to talk, Cornelius." Before he could turn, she moved around him to sit at her usual place at the table, placing her arms on the table, and looking up at him, he realized she had been crying. Uneasy and puzzled, he slowly sat down again, waiting for her to continue. "Something is going on with Henry. Doctor Murdock wants to talk to both of us, tomorrow when Henry's in school." Slowly and anxiously she repeated all that she knew and what the doctor had said, and he silently absorbed the seriousness of it all. Nodding his head, he asked what time they should leave the next day to meet Murdock.

Henry had left for school and was picked up at the bottom of the hill by a schoolmate whose parents took their own brood to school with horse and buggy. Cornelius and Lena were first in the doctor's office that morning after stopping at Stener and Gertie's to leave Clarence in their care. Choosing his words carefully Doctor Murdock explained what he believed to be "Ewing's Sarcoma". The constant low temperature, with leg pain aggravated by activity, and leg pain at night were symptoms which would become worse along with weight loss and fatigue. There was no cure. And the child would be at risk for bones breaking for no obvious reason. Whatever could be administered for pain--possibly opium, would be given. This was a disease that afflicted only young Caucasian males. Cornelius asked how much time Henry could live with the disease, and on hearing possibly two years, Lena's weeping was terrible. Their lives were to change drastically over the next two years.

When the weekend came, the parents sat down with Henry and talked with him about all that he was feeling, telling only what they thought he needed to know. Then answered his questions on the level of his understanding. They told him he would finish the school year, and then see if he felt well enough by fall to go on. If not, his lessons would continue at home with Mother's help.

The stress took its toll on Lena, and her labor began approximately two weeks earlier than expected. After backache and weak contractions that dragged on for two days, she went to the doctor. The baby's heartbeat was strong and regular, and Lena's vital signs all good, so she was sent home, assured the baby should arrive in 24 hours. She had made every last-minute preparation she could think of. What she had no control over was Cornelius and his obsession for a girl. After producing three boys, the odds were in favor of a fourth. Lena didn't choose any girl names.

On March 25, 1908 Lloyd Cornelius Erickson came wailing into Cornelius' world, unwanted. What made the baby's father so angry as he leaned close over this baby, taking in every feature of the infant? He sarcastically spat out--while throwing his hands up in disgust--"There's my girl!!?"

It was then Lena knew exactly what it was that Cornelius was set upon: a blond, blue-eyed girl! Lloyd had his mother's coloring and hair. Unfortunately, he didn't happen to be a girl and Cornelius never forgave him. Some things never change. But, then, Lena hadn't expected anything would.

At least while she was getting up with the baby and needing to nurse him, Lena could enjoy her time with her infant as Cornelius kept to himself upstairs. It no longer bothered her if her leaking, lactating, bleeding, sagging body repelled him.

That was HIS problem.

When Henry and Clarence met their new brother it was with hugs and kisses and laughter. They hovered over his cradle, and stroked the silky, blond curls as their mother rocked him. They asked to hold him, taking turns, and learned to be careful, supporting his head. Everyone loved the beautiful baby--except "Farr."

Even caring for a new baby didn't stop Lena's eyes from following Henry. Was he limping more? Was he showing signs of pain? Was he playing less? More tired? Many nights after nursing Lloyd and putting him in his cradle, she would silently climb the stairs, shielding a candle, to stand by Henry's bed, watching for any restlessness. Her heart ached for her son, even as she prayed for him.

Maybe it was the desperate hope a cure was just around the corner, that Lena was ready to try anything. In papers and magazines, advertisements abounded with the perfect cure for anything and everything. She had even made a poultice that was guaranteed to heal the most painful of joints. The instructions were to roll bread dough to the size of an egg. Then form the same size with old hog lard. Old lard worked better. Then work the two together till well blended. Then wrap around affected joint over night. It hadn't helped. Lena put all the things she heard or read to the doctor on the regular visits to him with Henry. And being a kind man, he always discounted the fake cures in ways that did not demean. He understood what Lena was going through.

Cornelius followed politics with great interest and held strong opinions. Especially when it came to women's rights and the suffragists. And especially Carrie Chapman Catt, who relentlessly pursued voting rights for women nationwide. President Theodore Roosevelt hadn't involved himself in women's issues, but he was in his eighth year as President and it was beginning to look like William Howard Taft might become the chosen successor of Roosevelt in 1908. And Cornelius became concerned Taft might take a different stance on women's rights. He had heard the man described as well-meaning and kind, even rather simple-minded. Cornelius also knew Lena's opinion on the subject though she refused to debate with him. She had a limited source of energy and she didn't waste it on closed minds.

From the moment Lena sat down at the piano and found she had not forgotten how to use the instrument, Henry had attached himself to her, dragging a chair in beside her, watching her hands with fascination. When she played songs, and sang, it wasn't long before he was singing them with her in his clear high voice, and she began to think he might like to learn. Clarence, who was Henry's shadow, followed, bringing whatever toy he found handy, and sat on the floor watching and listening.

Cornelius no longer harangued Lena to stop sissifying Henry, and no longer verbally pushed him to "toughen up."

Henry had finished his first year of school with no particular difficulty scholastically, but physically he lagged behind on the playground. He was small for his age and tired easily. He was glad when the summer came.

By September, the changes in Henry could not be missed and Lena was torn about letting him rejoin his class and friends. But Henry wanted to continue, so it was Cornelius who took the boy to school each morning and arranged for Lena to pick him up afterwards. The teacher was made fully aware of the advancing illness and became a dedicated protector for Henry, a bulwark between him and the playground bully. Henry would attend as long as he could safely do so. By the New Year, after their Christmas vacation, Henry was missing from his classroom-- but not forgotten. On the special days in each month, his teacher would deliver a large envelope filled with homemade Valentine cards, then St. Patrick cards, and Easter cards. Lena picked up his lesson assignments which she would go over with him Monday through Friday at the living room library table which had been converted to a desk for him. He worked at his studies diligently, resting frequently. He was a good reader, a bright student, but physically wasting away. He always had the low-grade fever; and pain that seemed to be everywhere by summer, making any activity unbearable, even with the doses of medicine prescribed by Doctor Murdock. During that last summer with Henry, Lena read many books to Henry. They seemed to have the power to lift him from his ruined body to places his mind was free. To reduce the risk of breaking Henry's bones during transfers from bed to downstairs, or to move him about when necessary, Dr. Murdock had fashioned a plaster cast form for Henry. It required Cornelius to carefully lift Henry into the midst of his family life as much as possible, while not inflicting more pain on him. His bones had begun the breaking process. Clarence followed with troubled eyes, never far from his brother, always careful now not to touch Henry. Lena arranged to have a photograph taken of Henry in his best outfit on his 8th birthday, September 4th.

Lena's Firstborn Son, Henry Orlando

Lena often slept on a cot in Henry's room now. On waking to a beautiful October morning, she knew as she looked at the fragile child, this day would be different. Assembling bath towels and warm water, she bathed her son and put a fresh white nightshirt on him, and Cornelius helped carry their son down the stairs to the parlor where the sun was now glowing through the stained glass windows, Henry's favorite room in the large house. And Cornelius carefully lifted the boy onto the quilt over Lena's lap and placed him in Lena's arms. Then he left, taking Clarence and Lloyd with him, to be left with the neighbors at the bottom of the hill. Then he left to bring the doctor.

As Lena rocked, she sang softly some of the songs she and Henry had sung together, and sometimes it was lullabies. She was singing "In the Hollow of His Hand" when Cornelius and the doctor entered the room. No one spoke as the doctor gently felt for pulse and listened for a heartbeat. When he shook his head, Lena kissed her son good-bye and delivered him into the hands that had delivered him into her hands only eight short years earlier. The young mortician waited in the kitchen.

Henry Orlando Erickson died October 12, 1908. Once again, Lena's dear sister-in-law was there to comfort and support, while hiding her own grief in not only losing a much-loved nephew but grieving over all the suffering that innocent child had to endure in his short life. "Praise be to God that was over." Belle felt sad that Lloyd at 15 months was too young to remember Henry, and she also felt sad that Clarence would. She knew the lonely boy cried himself to sleep at night.

Belle stayed several days, sleeping on Olga's cot, as it continued to be called, and helped Lena with visitors, and funeral arrangements. Burial would be in Highland Prairie. On her last night, Belle thought she heard the pad of bare feet on the stairs in the middle of the night and cautiously getting up peered around the doorway at the base of the stairs. There in the dim moonlight she saw the small figure sitting, leaning against the wall. Whispering, she spoke to him, "Clarence? Honey? What's wrong?" But she already knew. He didn't answer but was rubbing his fists into his wet eyes. It wasn't easy, but she managed to seat herself a step higher, and put a comforting arm around the small shoulders. "Are you missing Henry, Clarence?" A nod. "He's with Jesus now, and he doesn't hurt anymore." She knew he was listening intently. "Even though he's with Jesus, he still loves you. He would want you to know that. And he would not want you to go on feeling so sad when he is happy in Heaven. You think about that, honey--and how about you and I try to fit into Olga's cot and get some sleep? Tomorrow will be better."

Months passed and the routine of the living moved on. Fields still needed to be plowed, planted, and harvested. Gardens were still weeded and the produce preserved for the next season. Meals were still prepared and eaten, and "Big Bill Taft" was elected president. He was a pleasant, congenial man who accomplished very little, unless having the White House bathtub replaced with one large enough to hold his 340 pounds could be counted as an accomplishment. Cornelius was always especially jovial on the day he could cast his vote, knowing as he left, of the simmering resentment at being denied the voting privilege in his wife.

Lena was grateful for the comfort and visits of the family she had married into. Lena's sister-in-law, Carrie, came quite frequently with her son Hildus who was the same age as Clarence, and soon both boys would be in school. Clarence had slowly adjusted to Henry's absence and now Lloyd was attaching himself to his older brother just as Clarence had to Henry.

Sometimes Belle and Maren came when Carrie was there and the four women worked on the "hair art," under Belle's directions. Besides using their own hair, Lena had both Karen and Olga's hair. When Lena's neighbor, Gertie, learned of the project, she joined the group and proved to be especially skill-ful. These times were good for Lena, relaxing, fun, productive in fine stitchery and crocheting as well as "hair art".

Hildus and Clarence were enrolled in the 1910-11 school years but in different school districts. Clarence, as Henry had been, was acquainted with Sunday School friends, so enter-ing the world of school children was no problem, but Clarence soon discovered he was no longer free to go in or go out at will--and having to sit for long periods on a hard seat by an open window where all the beautiful outdoors could be seen proved too much. As he crawled over the windowsill, the teacher smacked his bottom with a paddle.

1911

A TIME TO EMBRACE AND A TIME TO REFRAIN

By January of 1911 Lena knew she was again expecting. In early June. She hadn't felt well for a few weeks, and suspecting the cause, had gone to see Doctor Murdock. Following his exam, he had spoken of his concern for the calcium loss he believed was occurring. He had noted that her back was no longer straight, and one hip was higher. He knew this would only get worse with time. When he asked her to open her mouth, she did so reluctantly; and he sighed after a thorough look with a light. Shaking his head regretfully, she heard him say, "It costs a tooth for every baby." She knew she needed to see a dentist, but for all her other strengths, Lena was terrified of dentists.

Once again, she left Cornelius to figure things out for himself. April arrived gently, earth greened up, and the birds were noisily building nests. The day the ladies had their spring tea in the church, Lena opted for a pleasant walk to the church. It wasn't that far actually. With Clarence in school, she had only three-year-old Lloyd, and he would enjoy the walk, might even work some excess energy out of him before the meeting. So she dressed her angelic looking son in his best clothes and shoes, and off they went. On leaving the yard, Lena paused, looking first at the lush green pasture, then the steep dirt drive leading to the dirt road going into town. Taking Lloyd by the hand, she put him through the fence, and then carefully got herself through. It was a beautiful walk, down the green sloping hill to the neighbor's yard. Lloyd was so happy, jumping and playing all the way across the pasture, then crawling under the fence all by himself, while Lena again carefully navigated the fence. And on they went to the church where Lena discovered, as Lloyd carefully climbed the high cement steps, that her son had stomped in every fresh cow-pie he saw on the way through the pasture.

The lovely month of April was slipping away too fast; and Cornelius, like all his neighbors, was going into the busy planting season. So when Lena saw a tired horse pulling a carriage past her kitchen window, she hurried to the back door where she recognized her sister-in-law's husband, Chris, as he came close and stopped. The horse's head drooped in weariness, and as Chris walked up to Lena, she knew from his face the news would not be good. "Is it Carrie? The boys?"

No, no--they are fine. And so are Maren and Belle. It's Hans. The doctor says it was his heart. I need to let Cornelius know."

"Cornelius is out in the field, but I will send the hired man out to tell him you need to talk with him. Care for your horse, and then come and tell me what has happened."

Seated in the kitchen with a cup of coffee in his hand, Chris relayed the events of the day to Lena. Hans had complained of not feeling well to Maren at breakfast and left his plate untouched. He'd said his kidneys had been hurting him all week. He'd left then to get the horses hitched up to begin field work. When he'd led the horses out of the barn, Belle saw him fall to the ground, unmoving. Rushing out, she knew he was gone, running back into the house, she called for the doctor.

On examining the body, the doctor believed Hans was dead before hitting the ground.

From that point on things just seemed to move so fast. Belle called Carrie, and then Herman, Emma, and Eric. Now funeral plans were underway.

Hans Erickson died April 27th, 1911. Burial was to be at Hesper. Lena grieved for Hans' family. He had been a good husband and father; he had always been so kind to her; and her children loved their gentle grandfather. He would be missed. All his children were expected for the funeral. Lena had met Herman and Hilda several times and liked them. Herman was an elegant, charming, friendly, personality, like Belle and Carrie. Eric and Martine she'd met once at Maren and Hans' home. They were expensively attired, polite, but distant, not easy to know. Emma and Birt she'd met several times and they were pleasant enough, but Emma was a lot like Eric, hard to know.

"How odd", Lena thought. "Six children raised by two loving parents, and three are fun-loving, open and nurturing. Three are closed and secretive. How very odd."

Change had to come for Maren and Belle. The farm was legally Maren's, but it was her three sons who decided what was to be done. By the grace of God, they were good men, and they made decisions that Maren agreed with: she and Belle would continue to live in their home, the land would be rented out, and Herman would oversee the financial side, with a set amount monthly for the two women's living expenses.

At least Hans had not suffered; he had reached his 76th year in good health, having enjoyed a contented life, and his death had come without sickness and suffering. There was much to be grateful for.

It seemed June would take forever in arriving. Lena was tired, out of sorts lately, and ready to be past the delivery. But the big day finally arrived, a beautiful June morning. Belle had been summoned and was on her way. The doctor had done the necessary exam and decided to wait this one out. This labor had the look of being quick when there were stronger contractions.

The doctor was a wise man. With the first really strong contraction, the water broke. In two more contractions, the head was crowning, and the doctor was hurriedly gathering sterile towels to catch the new arrival! A girl! Helen Gladys Erickson arrived June 6th, 1911. Belle washed and wrapped the crying baby, then cradled it lovingly until the doctor had finished up with Lena, then slowly placed the baby in the mother's arms. Cornelius had heard the words, "It's a girl," from the doctor while waiting in the living room. As soon as Belle exited the bedroom, he hurried in, leaned over the golden-haired infant, and with a joyful laugh, lifted the baby out of Lena's arms. He moved closer to the window to examine the baby more closely, and in a triumphant voice said, "This is my girl!"

A chill passed over Lena as she realized that all along only a blond female child was acceptable to Cornelius. But Lena wasn't the only person in the room looking with disbelief at the father. Doctor Murdock felt shocked as he remembered Cornelius' emotionless response to the four sons his wife had presented him, especially the reaction to the last boy. Blonde Lloyd. "What in God's name was wrong with the man!?" he wondered and felt pity for Lena. He hoped there would be no more births for the poor woman. He wondered why she had married the man in the first place. Dr. Murdock said his good-byes and departed for his office, with a feeling of depression. He treated many women and had seen so many signs of abuse. Bruises, broken ribs. And the women kept silent. It was always "just a fall." "Just clumsy." And he let them go, back to their abuser. A man could do as he pleased within his own four walls, even if it meant the woman died. Which had happened less than a year ago, when one of his patients died in a fall down her own cellar stairs. He had seen the yellowing older bruises, felt the lumpy ribs from old fractures, but no one could prove she didn't fall. The widower re-married immediately.

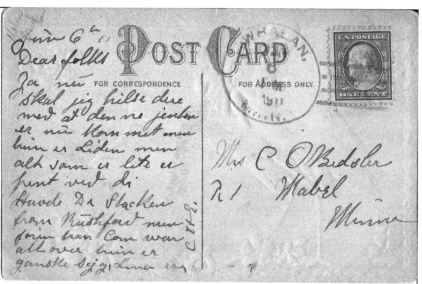

Birth Announcement for Lena's First Daughter, Helen Gladys

Helen Gladys Erickson, Cornelius' Favored Child

Cornelius' Baby Gift for Helen, a Vanity

Cornelius was exuberant over the birth of his daughter. And he did something he hadn't done for any of his sons at their birth, or at any other time afterwards either.

That very day he went into town and bought Helen a lovely oak dresser with a mirror. On returning home, he hauled it up the stairs, and put it in the bedroom he picked out for her. Two narrow bedrooms faced each other across the long hall, one on the north and one on the south. He put the dresser into the one on the south, between the stairway and Cornelius' room. He never tried to hide his favoritism; he simply didn't care how his sons felt in his disregard for them. And Lena could do nothing about it. He showed no interest in them, didn't bother to converse pleasantly and spoke harshly. But Helen he carried around every chance he had, with smiles and sweet talk. By the time she could toddle, he would put her on his shoulder and go into town to show off his beautiful blonde daughter. Lena treated all her children the same, including Helen. But she was especially protective and sheltering of her sons, permitting no violence against them. Cornelius knew not to cross that line, though he insisted they do chores. He was harsh in word and expectations. Lena did her best to help them learn how to navigate the rough passage they had with their father.

They were a family that attended church regularly. The children had Sunday school, memorized Bible verses, and songs. Lena had prayer with them in the home and instilled a lifelong faith in all her children.

It was Clarence who revealed why there was never more than the one cat on the farm: Cornelius killed the kittens when he found them and fed them to the pigs. It bothered Clarence to the point of nightmares. Lena seldom confronted her husband on anything. She believed there were things too important to let go, but knowing her husband, she carefully picked her battles. Neither Clarence nor Lloyd ever witnessed or was pushed to participate in the kitten slaughters.

One kitten would be regularly left with the mother.

Helen was two when Lloyd started school; she was too young to understand why she was alone, and became a little clingy for awhile, but Lena enjoyed the quiet time with her daughter, taking her along as she worked, often carrying her on a hip.

Belle had grown so attached to the tiny girl that her visits had increased in frequency and she had every intention of spoiling her niece. Maren never stayed behind and Carrie took to popping in to see everyone at once, with her one-year-old Bernie in tow. Now Belle had two little ones to enjoy spoiling. There were many such pleasant days when Helen and Bernie were small, and the four women laughed, shared stories, and enjoyed tea and cookies.

The day of the tornado was just before Helen's fifth birthday. Clear skies and what started as a lovely day, heated up quite fast, making it hot in the house, but something felt different as the day passed. A stillness and silence came, then a darkening, and a coolness of the air. Alarmed, Lena raced through the house closing windows and doors as fast as she could. It was dark--really dark now, and a wind was whipping the one large old tree in the front yard, seemingly in all directions. Helen followed fast on Lena's heels, upset, but not knowing why; and then in the almost-night-darkness came the howling roar of wind, and the house seemed to shudder. Creaking could be heard; the living room door shook and rattled until Lena, in panic, thought it would be blown open. She had grabbed a quilt from her bed and raced to the door and in a hopeless effort held the blanket over the door edges with all her strength, and flattened her thin frame against the shaking wood, as Helen watched. Then as fast as it had come, the monster was gone.

Weak-kneed and trembling, Lena dropped the quilt on the floor, and slowly holding Helen's hand, they walked through the house out the back door. The barn and buildings seemed battered but were still standing. The beautiful old tree was not; there had been three at one time, and now none. Turning towards the house, and looking upwards, Lena could see numerous shingles missing from the roof. The rugs that had still been drying on the clothesline were gone. Looking east towards town, Lena gasped, and clamped a hand over her mouth--the neighbor's house was gone. Hurrying now along the west side of the house and looking down hill--she felt light-headed--another house was gone, too! Her stomach churned. It was as if the tornado had dipped into the valley on one side, lifted up over their home and dipped back down on the other.

It had been a bad tornado, and had done a lot of damage, but no one's life was lost and it passed by on the edge of Mabel. Helen never forgot seeing her mother trying to hold a tornado out with the blanket. No one ever bothered to plant another tree.

Times were simpler then, and fun was found in simple things. In the winters, the hill in the pasture was perfect for winter sports, and Lena made sure the children had sleds, skis, and a toboggan. She ripped and turned adults old winter wear and sewed warm coats and pants for them. She knit scarves, mittens, and hats. Her children never lacked the necessities. In town was an ice rink where they could ice skate when they were old enough to go by themselves, carrying their strap-on skates. A bonfire was always lit near the rink for warming cold fingers and toes. When spring and summer came, Lena's children played "King of the Mountain" on the great rock, later known as a "cabbage rock."

Helen Pictured on Cabbage Rock

Their Bidsler cousins and town friends frequently joined the fun. The apple orchard was another pleasant place to hang out. They climbed the low branches, where a swing was hung up. And in the fall, they ate apples. Perhaps it was because Lena expended all her attention on her children that she did not bother with any particular interior decorating. Getting money from Cornelius may have been a big factor. Other than the one big bedroom that had been Henry's which did get papered years later, the evidence in all the other rooms throughout the house was that no changes were made after Lena moved in and slowly the wallpaper faded and darkened to the point that each room had a gray dismal appearance. Curtains weren't bothered with upstairs, or in the parlor, music room or kitchens. Lace curtains hung in Lena's bedroom and on the one window in the dark living room. Neither did she bother with new furniture other than more chairs. She did set the two plant stands Clarence and Lloyd made in high school in front of the single living room window and placed a large fern on the tallest stand. The only other piece of furniture was Cornelius' grandfather clock which would sit at the base of the stairs as long as he lived. She seemed to have no interest in possessions. Books were another matter; she encouraged her children to read and sing together. Clarence in particular carried a good tune, had a good memory, and wasn't shy in singing lustily. Helen learned to play the piano from a young man, John Bates, who traveled from house to house giving piano lessons for 20-25 cents.

Picture-taking days were always looked forward to by everyone. Lena and Carrie had established the custom of posing Clarence and Hildus together in similar outfits every five years. They accomplished their goal the 5th, 10th, and 15th year, but by 20 the young men had other interests. Odd, that for all the enjoyment and anticipation of the families getting together for keepsake photographs, smiles seem to be forbidden.

And of course, Helen had a doll which Lena sewed clothes for out of leftover fabric. No material was ever wasted. A really fine gown was fashioned for the doll from leftover fine muslin from the baptismal gown. And Helen stained the neck with milk trying to feed the baby doll. That little doll dress would still be around over 100 years later, with a ribbon added to hide the milk stain.

"Seasons come and seasons go, but some things never change" was running through Lena's mind as once again she waited for the doctor in his exam room. She already knew what the signs meant, and she prayed for another girl; one that would serve to humble Helen. No one was blind to Cornelius' favoritism among his children. And it was not good for anyone. After Helen had proudly announced to her mother a few days earlier that she was "Pa's favorite," Lena had lectured her on unattractive pride, and that it was just Pa's way of saying--"How nice to have a girl, finally."

Cousins: Hildus and Clarence

Helen's Doll Dress Handmade by Lena

1917

A TIME TO KEEP AND A TIME TO CAST AWAY

Her thoughts had wandered as she waited, so she startled as the door opened briskly and the graying kindly doctor entered. Whether from her expression, or he had already surmised the reason for her visit, he stopped in front of her, and half smiling, half serious, shook his head, "You are not getting younger, Lena. Tell Cornelius to start sleeping in the barn." He knew from his exam of Lena her health had slipped more, but what could he do? He agreed with her in thinking the first week in May would be the delivery date. As she left, he told her to eat more, and rest more. She did neither. And she didn't tell Cornelius. Why change what works? She quietly once again prepared what was needed for another baby, and for the home delivery, praying all would go well, grateful for the loyal Belle who would run the household until she was on her feet again. And it was good that Helen would turn six years old two months after the baby was born and be starting school in the fall. The boys were growing so fast--8 and 11 already and growing more independent by the day. The day would come when Cornelius would have no hold over them –that would be a good day. Sometimes she wondered as she sat in church with her well-groomed, well-behaved children, next to the faithful, church-going husband-father; what was the impression left in the minds of observers? Everything just appeared so perfect. Only she knew it wasn't. She prayed constantly for forgiveness of her anger and the ever-present bitterness.

Lena's rest during the night was broken, and she finally got up, pre-dawn, having given up on falling back asleep. She was tired, the house felt cold, and she struggled with the cook stove trying to get a fire going. It was slow starting, finally beginning to crackle and warm the cold metal by the time she had filled the large enamel coffee pot and set the grounds keeper into it. She needed a nice, hot cup of coffee. While it heated to a percolating stage, she returned to her room to dress for the day, adding an old sweater to her attire for warmth. She heard Cornelius coming down the stairs as she waited for the grounds to settle before pouring herself a cup of coffee. She had warmed the cups on the warming shelf over the stove, and now took down the ugly mustache cup for Cornelius, filled and set it on the table for him. As she stood by the warm stove, she felt the tightening gently beginning across her lower back, spreading and tightening across her stomach, then fade away. Now she quietly waited. It was still April, with several weeks to go before the time of expected confinement. But, remembering Lloyd had come two weeks early, maybe this one was to be early, too. It was only two, or a little more, weeks early--things should be fine.

Then the second contraction began, very much the same as the first, and she knew she would need to change her plans for the day. Cornelius listened silently as she told him of the impending labor, then he, too, began re-arranging his day. He got Clarence up to begin chores while he contacted the doctor. Clarence, at 11, already knew the care and feeding of the livestock. It was a hurried cold breakfast for Clarence and Cornelius, and then each left to take care of what needed to be done. Cornelius on his return told Lena he had used the doctor's phone to call Belle, who should arrive mid-morning, if not sooner, and the doctor would be coming by to determine progress shortly. Lena put her kitchen back in order and then began setting up her room for the soon-to-be delivery. While preparing the cradle, she felt a warm trickle starting and knew change could happen fast. She wished the doctor were here. Swiftly, she undressed and put on a clean night dress, then returned to her bed to wait.

Her relief on seeing the doctor was great, and on examination of the patient, the leaking membrane ruptured. "Lena, you've always been really considerate in not keeping us waiting, so I'll just help myself to some of that coffee I smelled on my way in and hang out in your kitchen for awhile. Okay with you?"

Lena smiled one of her rare smiles at the kind doctor and settled down to being considerate once again.

Belle barely made it in time for the birth, having first seated Maren in the kitchen with a cup of cream and sugar laden coffee, before hurrying into the bedroom to see the red-haired head resting in the doctor's hand, guiding the infant's body onto sterile towels, where he rubbed the baby dry, causing outraged screams and waving clenched fists at such treatment from the new family member.

Cornelius waited in the living room, listening, but a beaming Belle poked her head out, announcing, "It's a girl."

A satisfied gleam appeared in his eyes, and his mouth curved in a smile.

Lena breathed a "thank you" and cradled her baby as the doctor finished his work. She stroked the curling red hair, and stared into the very dark blue eyes, and was sure they would turn brown in time--and thought of the beloved Olga of her childhood--her sister.

The doctor congratulated both parents as Cornelius finally entered the room and acknowledged the doctor's words before going to the side of the bed to see his new daughter for the first time. He seemed unaware of the eyes of the two others in the room. Belle had gone to tell Maren the news. Cornelius leaned close to the resting infant, looking hard at the red hair and the features. Cornelius' smile was gone, his small eyes expressionless. And both Lena and the doctor knew if the child had been blonde she would not have been rejected. In that moment, Lena knew what name she wanted for her beautiful red-haired daughter.

Olga Christena Erickson was born April 20, 1917.

Cornelius went to take care of his farm while Belle set about fixing lunch. Helen was in the bedroom "oh-ing and ah-ing" over what she came to feel was her own living doll. Lloyd hovered close over the new addition, putting his little finger in the baby's palm, and laughing to feel the tiny fingers close on his.

Both children soon headed for the kitchen for food and spoiling. Helen's words floated back to Lena, "Aunt Belle's my favorite aunt." And Lloyd's voice came saying, "I wonder which of us gets the dime." The dime was in a pocket of Maren's dress where it would have been for---no one knew how long. The blind grandmother always had one hidden there that she rubbed between her fingers for long stretches of time sitting in darkness, and when it would eventually come out, to be placed in the hand of a lucky grandchild, it glowed like sterling silver. Today the child was Clarence--perhaps because he was doing chores while the others were rejoicing.

Helen had no contender for the position of "Pa's" favorite. Cornelius favored Helen, and only Helen. But the sweet-natured little red-haired girl won the hearts of everyone else.

The bond of extended family was important for Lena and her children, with play for the young cousins and closeness for Lena with her in-laws. Aunt Carrie and Uncle Chris came with their sons, Hildus and little brother, Bernie. Clarence being the same age as Hildus particularly looked forward to the visits. It was good for Carrie's sons to be in the busy Erickson household as both Bernie and Hildus clung so close to their mother that being out of her presence caused them to cry with fear. They struggled to adapt when they became of school age.

Fall came again, and school dictated the daily routine of all the children, many of whom would sooner or later come home with sniffles and sneezes. But for Bernie, it was always the sore throat, and missing school to recover till Carrie agreed it was necessary for the seven-year-old to have the tonsillectomy. It had been difficult the first year getting the shy boy into school where he cried, day after day for his mother. Carrie had cried at home, and the teacher had been at her wit's end in the classroom. It seemed the child had no sooner given up crying in his second year of school than he was told he'd need an operation, and his anxiety hit new levels all over again in spite of his mother's reassurance she would be right there with him.

On the scheduled day for the surgery both parents arrived at the small hospital with Bernie gripping his mother's hand. He resisted the nurses getting him ready for surgery and clung to Carrie. She helped the crying boy onto the gurney, holding his hand as he was wheeled through the halls, begging her not to leave him, and she promised to stay right beside him until it was over.

He said, "You promise?"

And she'd answered, "Yes," expecting to be at his side until he was under the anesthetic. But as the gurney reached the double doors of the surgery with doctor, anesthetist and two nurses waiting, Carrie was abruptly separated from Bernie. Her last memory of him was of Bernie sitting upright, arms reaching towards her, his mouth open, screaming. Seven-year-old Bernie died on the operating table. Carrie claimed he died of fear. The doctor had no explanation; and Carrie never forgave the people in that surgery.

After that Carrie kept Hildus even closer than she had kept both her sons before Bernie's death. Hildus, too, had suffered under any separation from his mother, and as time passed, he became shyer and more reclusive. He never left the tiny home in Prosper, Minnesota where he'd been born. But years later, on a warm day when open windows cooled the rooms, a lucky passerby would hear violin music of haunting beauty being played for the ears of the musician alone.

And I've gotten ahead of myself (probably not for the first time!) Bernie's death was a shock to the family. Carrie's sons were quiet, gentle boys, and much-loved by their cousins, as well as by their elders. Helen seemed the most distressed and thought God was mean. Lena told her "heaven wouldn't be perfect without children", and that made sense to the young girl. Now, Lena returned as much kindness to Carrie as she herself had received from her sister-in-law in her own terrible times of loss.

As 1917 faded into 1918, Lena felt very much under the weather, pushing herself to get up--dragging through the day, trying to care for baby Olga, trying to nurse her, but having to finally resort to a baby formula from the drug store. As months dragged on, and then April arrived, word of the Spanish Flu becoming a worldwide epidemic was spreading fast, and Lena feared that must be what was happening to her, but she knew of no one around her having it--but then feared perhaps she was maybe first. And then again, it could possibly be her age. She was spotting again; everything had been "off," going on close to maybe five months. Maybe it was time to take her complaints to the doctor. Perhaps the next week she'd make an appointment. Now she reached down and scooped up her plump baby sitting on a blanket on the floor, trying to fit spoons and wooden blocks into her mouth. Olga liked to sit, but still toppled over easy, and then had trouble righting herself.

Holding the baby to one hip, Lena moved from stove to cupboard to table. Back and forth hurrying to put lunch on the table. Cornelius would be coming in very soon for his meal. She shoved a lift-handle into a stove lid and set it to the side, preparing to add wood from the wood box. Then twisting while bending to keep Olga secure, she lifted the chunk of wood, and simultaneously felt a searing pain across her low abdomen. Dropping the wood but clutching the baby she staggered back with a shrill "Ahhhh"—filling the room.

Olga's bright head jerked back, round startled eyes went to her mother's face and the lower lip quivered as the eyes filled with tears.

Lena needed to lie down, but the fire had to be covered, and she managed that, then moved slowly to her bed, easing down to sit on the edge before sliding Olga to a sitting position on the floor. Praying for Cornelius to come and help her, she lay flat on her bed on top of her quilt, knowing what was happening--Pregnant. Again!--and she hadn't figured it out? How, in the name of Heaven, could she not have known? She felt something trying to slip out of her own body and reaching down endeavored to remove her undergarments. Blood. Pain. Then something still and silent lay on the quilt between her thighs. She thought she saw one small movement as if a breath was attempted. The eyes remained closed.

She heard Cornelius in the kitchen and screamed his name, then heard him running through the living room.

By now Olga was crying as though her heart was breaking.

Cornelius looked shocked, disbelieving.

"Go! Get the doctor, Cornelius!"

He turned to leave, then stopped, "Isn't he at the hospital, in Rushford? Checking his patients?"

Before she could respond she felt the pain of the placenta releasing and then, it too, was on the bed. "Towels--get me towels, hurry." With her hands she did what Dr. Murdock had done for the bleeding. She massaged the now-empty uterus, making it clamp down. And tears ran down her face as she looked at the small motionless form. She didn't know how many months it was; so tiny--four months, maybe? Or five? She didn't know if it was male or female.

Stemming the bleeding with one towel and more massage, she opened a second towel and gently placed the tiny body on it, trying to gently dry the delicate skin, looking for signs, any sign of life, and could discern none.

Cornelius watched helplessly, and Olga sobbed. Lena carefully wrapped the tiny stillborn in the towel along with the placenta. There would be no funeral.

Looking at Cornelius she said, "Please, pick up Olga and comfort her." Then she added, "I don't think we should upset the children, and they will be home soon."

And he answered. "I will bury it before they are back from school." Coming round the bed, he set Olga down and reached for the bundle, folding the towel over the face.

"In the apple orchard, Cornelius. Under the center tree at the top of the hill.

Cornelius nodded in agreement. Then left with the sad little bundle.

The tears seemed to seep from her eyes, she couldn't stop them. Looking at Olga, she wondered how she was going to manage but what choices were there? Slowly she rose, pressing a fresh towel into service, and re-dressed. She wanted to watch the lonely burial under the apple tree. Making her way slowly through the parlor to the music room window, knowing that Olga, in spite of her wailing would be alright for a few minutes, she stood at the window and looked toward the orchard where apple blossoms glowed white, beyond and past the pigpen, looking for Cornelius under the tree. She froze, her eyes shot back to the fence at the pigpen and stared at Cornelius, with arms resting on the board fence, one foot propped up, watching his pigs eating. And she knew.

Shaking, weak, trying to process her thoughts, the helpless cries of Olga brought her back to the bedroom where as carefully as she could, she picked up Olga, and then sat in the small arm-less rocker in the corner of the room. And waited, thinking.

She couldn't bring herself to look at the face of the man she'd married. She had tried to make the marriage work in the beginning and had continued to try for years. It had been all for nothing; Cornelius was what he was. A cold, self-centered man. But what she had witnessed, what she believed--unshakably--to have happened, could not be undone.

He had come back into the room, and stood watching her, not missing the white face and clenched lips, but erroneously attributed her frozen face and posture to what she had just gone through.

When she spoke it was low, and expressionless, "The chil-dren will be coming soon. Put all the stained bedding in a bun-dle and hide it in the dressing room."

As soon as that was done she asked him to warm a bottle of milk for Olga. When he returned with a warmed bottle--much to her surprise that he had accomplished the seemingly simple task for the daughter he could completely ignore--she then told him she felt too ill to do anything and to please go for Belle.

While he was gone, her energetic, hungry children came in from school, bringing normalcy with them, and called out for her, not finding her in the kitchen with bread-with-jam, and a glass of milk waiting. Hearing her voice from the bed-room they crowded in, and seeing her pallor, were silent and anxious. She forced a small smile, and in as normal a voice as she could, explained simply that she really was feeling under the weather but Pa had gone for Belle. Now she needed them to help her as well by making for themselves, their own bread and jam. And they could even help themselves to one cookie each. Only one. And the mood lifted immediately.

Calling Clarence back, she asked if he would mind, after his snack, to take care of the chickens for her.

Listening to their voices in the kitchen gave Lena a sense of peace. When Belle arrived, so did order and comfort, but

Lena didn't tell her what her brother had done. That good and loving sister did not need to know that about him. By nightfall, all was as it should be except for Lena's thoughts and plans. First she had to recover and get her health back.

She felt better in several days, but this time she took a full two weeks to gather strength. By the end of May she felt the best she had in a long time, and now she began to carry forward with plans, but only after she had walked through the apple orchard making a thorough search for a small grave.

Already she was seeing Cornelius' inclination to return to her bed, but Lena was through with acquiescence for the sake of peace, and avoidance, of the mental retribution and meanness he meted out.

In the time Olga napped, with the others all in school, Lena emptied every item belonging to Cornelius from what was to be her room--hers alone--to his private upstairs room. Bit by bit she carried it all upstairs and left it on his bed. And she thought to herself, the barn was more fitting for him, as the doctor had suggested several years earlier.

The man had more in common with animals than humans. It was an ugly scene when Cornelius realized what Lena had done. She never raised her voice or argued with him and nothing he said to her mattered.

The truth was, her icy immovability raised fear in him. But still he believed he could break her down.

She no longer looked into the despised face, but always past his shoulder or at some other point.

To end the dreadful conflict, she quietly asked him to walk her to the small grave under the apple tree, and then she did stare him in the eyes in utter silence.

He looked at the floor, then turned and left. He kept to his own room from then on.

But, true-to-form, he punished her. The boys were given the jobs of filling the wood box and bringing in all the household water, as well as carrying out the slop water. He knew he could hurt her most through the children. Lena's favorite cat--Mitzi--disappeared.

As if the chasm in the family weren't enough, the Spanish Flu ran rampant throughout the country, bringing with it such fear, sickness, death, and untold misery as to be indescribable. Farmers were a little more protected by their isolation. Also they provided their own food so were never hungry, with some left over to share or sell. Lena's eggs sold for 21-cents a dozen. A half-gallon of milk brought 14-cents, as did 10 pounds of potatoes.

It was a hardship for two years. And it took two lives in the Erickson family. Cornelius' brother, Eric, in the fall of 1919 was dead at 50 years of age. And Ole, Lena's father.

News of Ole's death came in 1920 as spring was arriving. The local sheriff appeared early enough in the morning at the Erickson's door to be able to talk to both Lena and Cornelius. He was invited in and offered a chair, and coffee. The coffee he refused. He told them no one had checked on Ole for weeks, partly because of influenza and partly because he was known to keep to himself. Due to the low temperatures, there had been little decomposition, but the evidence was there: he had died of influenza. So the burial had been hasty, and his church held a small service.

When the scourge was ended a memorial was planned in memory of those lost from January 1918 to December 1920.

As the sheriff was giving his report to Lena, a small girl--maybe three years old--with a mop of red curls wandered into the kitchen and came for a closer look at the visitor and stumbled over the man's feet. He was quick to catch her and set her upright, thinking "what a little charmer."

Having offered his regrets, he rose to leave, escorted by the family. Pausing at the door, with a nod to Cornelius, he was just in time to see the small girl fall over a pail near an old stove. She picked herself up with no crying, but rubbing an elbow, while Lena remarked, "She will grow out of her clumsiness."

1920

A TIME TO REND AND
A TIME TO SEW

They lived in an armed camp of two contenders, where gloves would come off after the last child left home--glad to be gone. But at this time the couple co-existed under the same roof, following the routines established around children, farm work, meals, and church. Always keeping the masks in place for any outsiders. And Cornelius kept to his own room upstairs.

Cornelius had expected to get his hands on the Hogenson farm at Ole's death, and for all intents and purposes, he succeeded. The farm was left to Lena but was then sold and the money went into an account bearing both names, but Lena never saw a cent. Cornelius paid off his farm.

Clarence graduated from high school that spring, and began seeking employment in town, while still living and working at home. And the three others started school in September where one of them came home with something contagious--mumps, which spread to all four children. Olga and Helen being younger weren't as sick, recovered faster and were witness to how sick Clarence and Lloyd were, with temperatures to the point of delirium. They were found wandering outdoors in their underwear, shocking Helen. The mumps had gone down on the boys. Cornelius Erickson's line ended. Not that he cared.

Two events that were good occurred before the year 1920 ended. The first was when Olga started school and the teacher reported to Lena that Olga needed glasses. Olga wasn't clumsy after all; she just couldn't see. And Lena wondered how she could have missed the evidence; bumping into walls, bouncing off door jambs, tipping over cups and tumblers, things buttoned wrong. So many signs.

The eye doctor verified the teacher's observation and, after the exam, glasses were ordered. On the day Olga went to have the glasses fitted at the doctor's office, she reacted in astonishment, pointing to a clock on the wall and exclaiming, "It has numbers on it!" It was a whole new world to her. And best of all, she wasn't clumsy anymore.

The second event was a long awaited one, a more than 50-year longed-for day by women refusing to be refused their God-given right to vote equally with men. Sadly, the woman, Carrie Chapman Catt, who led the organization and who had marched repeatedly for women's rights died one year before. President Wilson, in his last year of presidency, signed the Women's Voting Rights Act into law. He had favored the rights of women the eight years he was President, but was a peaceable man, disliking contention so he waited until he was on his way out to sign it into law.

Lena voted for the first time when she was 42 years old--determined to do so. Cornelius inwardly fumed but had no voice. She was dressed and ready, waiting in front of the barn as he brought the horse and carriage out. He would have left without her--which she had already figured out.

She didn't discuss who she voted for--Warren G. Harding, a Republican, or James Cox, a Democrat. Not knowing who Cornelius was for, she thought it wise to remain silent. As it turned out, Harding was elected.

The female voter turn-out of the town and surrounding

area was astonishing. And seeing them arriving to cast their votes was especially galling to Cornelius. He believed bad days were ahead for men now that women had taken the reins in their hands. Now there would be no stopping them. And what did women know of government and law anyway?

Lena said very little about her painful back but had talked to the new doctor in town. She missed Dr. Murdock, who had died peacefully in his sleep, but was grateful the good man hadn't suffered. The new doctor only told her the deterioration would be progressive. A firm, elasticized support might afford some relief. A seamstress in town had tried to fit her with a vest-like garment that helped but was so hot in warm weather. She'd had to resort to wearing glasses now, too. She was beginning to feel the wear and tear of the years on her body.

The sun felt so good while she sat on her bench shelling peas as the sun moved to the west. How many hours, days, of her life had passed as she sat on this bench, cleaning vegetables, cleaning chickens for meals, churning butter? She thought about the house, how little it meant to her. So little, she'd never wanted to fix it up, to really clean it, paper, paint. Cornelius would never have parted with the money anyway without a fight. It wasn't worth the struggle. Besides the more she sat while doing her work, the easier it was on her back. That probably also contributed to her lack of interest. While sewing clothes for her children she could sit. And she sat as much as she could while cooking. Now as she finished the peas, she raised her head, and leaning back against the wall of the house, her eyes took in the hated pig fence, and a dark place in her mind formed the thought, "Cornelius and his house can go to hell for all I care."

A commotion was going on somewhere in the house. She could hear Helen's raised voice, demanding something, followed by an angry response from Olga. And then double footfalls were coming rapidly nearer until the screen door flew open, and a disheveled Olga banged out followed closely by Helen with a comb in her hand. Waving it and loudly complaining that Olga wouldn't stand still to have her hair combed. Now the angry girl spun towards her mother, accusing her sister of deliberately pulling her hair and she didn't have to put up with it. With a tired sigh, Lena looked at her girls and said, "I asked Helen to comb your hair before we eat. It looks like a rat's nest. Now let her do that. And Helen, be as gentle as you can."

Helen moved again towards Olga and began once more to comb out tangles. Something pulled--again--and Olga yowled and jerked away. Up came the thick, hard comb in Helen's hand, then down again with a "thwack"--and a cracking sound. Lena's best comb was now in two pieces, and Olga began howling for good reason.

As the children grew they did become more independent. And Lena grew more dependent on help from them. Clarence went about his chores without saying much. He was quiet, thoughtful, and contemplative, whereas, Lloyd tended towards outspokenness, with signs of control issues, which worried Lena. She prayed he would not be like his father, and she talked to him with patient gentleness, building a closeness and mutual respect with her handsome young son.

Belle's and Maren's visits were becoming further apart as signs of Maren's increasing feebleness became more evident. It was not unexpected when word came of Maren's passing on March 25th, 1925, but her loss was deeply felt by all her family. Her gentle presence was greatly missed. Olga, who had become the most frequent recipient of the polished dime, cried the hardest.

One vice that hadn't reared its ugly head in any of Lena's or Cornelius' extended families, or in their own, was that of alcohol. But the Roaring 20's was in full bloom and liquor was liberally consumed everywhere. There was no evidence that Clarence and Lloyd were indulging, but they enjoyed evenings out with friends in town. Keeping secrets in a small town would be an exception, and Lloyd would be no exception. For one thing, he stood out among his peers. He was 6'3", slender, but broad-shouldered, handsome. And his blond curly hair earned him the nickname "Tops." He appeared outgoing, self-assured, was opinionated—some thought pushy. He was seen in the popular beer hall, and seen inebriated on a number of occasions, but one time was gossiped about. He had become confrontational with the barkeeper. A young woman had accompanied him in that evening, and as she tried to convince Lloyd it was time to leave, he had shoved her. The sheriff was then called and Lloyd sobered up in the jail cell. A wiser, repentant Lloyd was allowed to leave pre-dawn to spare his respectable parents the shame and embarrassment.

Lena was wakened from deep sleep late in the night to find Lloyd on his knees at her bedside, his head bowed with his face in his hands. All he said was, "Forgive me, Mother." Her response was a soft, simple "I forgive you," with her hand resting on his head. That was all. He left. she never questioned him, and he lived a clean, self-disciplined life. He never married but looked after his mother the rest of her life.

It fell to Helen to care for the chickens and clean the coop, a job she hated, and complained often about. The filthiness of the chickens was almost more than she could bear, and she was frequently vocal about it. Lena's patient response never changed; "Life is full of dirty messes. Just dig in, and get the job done."

Lena knew teen children could be moody, challenging; and dealing with them took careful navigating. Olga had changed from happy to moody and resentful, eventually confronting her mother in the midst of kneading bread in the pantry. "I look just like him, don't I, Ma? Like Pa! That's why everybody hates me." And then the tears followed.

Lena could think of nothing to say; so she carefully began cleaning her hands of dough and flour. She knew the boys ignored their sisters, but for different reasons: Helen was pampered by Cornelius; and Olga--it was true--looked like her father. Lena knew Cornelius was a very bad father. "You look like yourself, Olga. And it's natural to have hair the color of one or the other of your parents. Your hair is the color of your Pa's, but also of your beautiful Aunt Olga. God made you as you are." And then she put her arms around her daughter in a warm hug. As it turned out, Lena raised four fine young people by the grace of God.

1923--The Harding Presidency was the most scandalous in presidential history. When he died from tainted food two years into his term of office, his V.P., Calvin Coolidge, finished out the next two years, quietly cleaning up the mess, and sent the guilty parties to the courts to be dealt with. Coolidge was re-elected for the next four years. And the Roaring Twenties roared on. America wallowed in booze, corruption, and over-indulgence right up to August 1929 when the music died--and the Great Depression descended. In 1929, Herbert Hoover was sworn in as president and in October the Stock Market crashed. Men jumped from skyscrapers, unable to face financial ruin. The Money-God had failed them. The Great Depression dragged on for forty-three terrible months.

The New Deal was launched by President Franklin Delano Roosevelt in 1933, and between April 5th and July 1st had the CCC in action putting 300,000 young men to work building bridges, parks, and roads. The New Deal was a new beginning. Two of the young men put to work on roads outside Mabel would become Lena and Cornelius' sons-in-laws. Ray and Bud Kephart, brothers from Hampton, a small town north of Waterloo.

Helen attended Teacher's College in Winona, Minnesota following graduation. She wanted to go into nursing but was forbidden by Cornelius who said, "It is indecent for young women to be giving men bed baths. No daughter of mine will be a nurse." So Helen attended Teacher's College for two years and did her practice teaching.

In the winter of '33 she met the lively, good-looking Ray Kephart one weekend in town, and that was when Lloyd's control issues took over. He deemed Ray not good enough for his sister, and remained constant in his disapproval, going so far as to forbid her to see him; and ordering Ray off the property.

What made things worse was the bad news that the new road would be changed from the one at the base of the hill and would instead cut straight through the Erickson wheat field and pass on the north side of Mabel. That raised quite a storm with several farms, but right-of-way was taken for almost nothing in return.

As to Lloyd's dislike of Ray, he never said, but hindsight can sometimes expose things that should have been dealt with sooner rather than later. Lloyd never openly revealed to his family he enjoyed sipping on two beers every Saturday night. Just two. As he said to a niece years later, "I have no problem with a man handling the bottle. Just not the bottle handling the man." Lloyd had seen Ray on Saturday nights being "handled by the bottle."

To reveal that would expose his own attendance in the low establishments.

Between being bossed by her brother, and not really wanting to teach, it took Helen two months of having met Ray to the couple getting married by a Justice of the Peace, April 24th, 1934. To add to Lloyd's trouble in trying to drive Ray off, Olga at sixteen thought Ray's older brother, Bud (a.k.a. Jake) was just the most handsome man she'd ever seen.

Lena's family was changing. Helen had married and moved out, and Clarence had gone to Minot, North Dakota looking for work. The Great Depression ended in March of 1933, and jobs were coming back. Lloyd worked on the farm along with Cornelius, who never got over having to cross the highway to get to the rest of his land.

With Helen's marriage, Ray's six siblings all, sooner or later, met all the Ericksons, so it was no surprise that Olga's heart was set on "Jake."

Lena's first grandchild arrived on St. Patrick's Day the following year--two months premature. Helen and Ray had gone for a nice Sunday ride in their new (to them) Model T on unpaved roads with deep potholes. On hitting a bad one, Helen was bounced so hard her head hit the roof of the car, slamming her back to the hard cushion rupturing the amniotic sac. Tiny Jason was born in the doctor's office. It would be summer before Lena would hold the infant that could fit in a shoebox when he was born.

Ray and Jake were smokers, and Olga secretly took up the habit. When she turned 19 in 1936, there was no talking her out of marrying Jake and they eloped. Cornelius had refused to pay for any continuing education for Olga, saying, "Education is a waste of money on girls. Look at Helen. All wasted money and time."

As for Lloyd, he never accepted the Kephart brothers as good enough for his sisters, and actually pushed Olga off the porch when the newlyweds returned with their news.

There would eventually be five grandchildren for Lena. Cornelius showed no interest. News of the premature birth of Jason had stressed Lena. Old memories returned to haunt her and she worried over Helen until the day his mother, Helen arrived and placed him in his grandmother's arms. For having been such a loving mother to all her children in such an unhealthy atmosphere, Lena wasn't much of a grandmother, never visiting any of them in their homes. There was never a Christmas or birthday gift. She only rarely spoke to them. But then, there was still a hanging on of an old saying of, "Children should be seen and not heard."

Although she never visited any of the 10 or more houses Helen and Ray regularly moved into and out of, she quite obviously loved seeing her daughters when they showed up. Olga and Jake lived in Waterloo, Iowa where Jake was a truck driver. Ray was a welder-harness maker and mechanic in different towns.

Perhaps Lena would have been more welcoming of the first two grand daughters born in May and December if the first hadn't been such a disappointment. Linda was born with grossly bowed legs. On seeing her, Lena was taken aback, to say the least. Added to that, the child frowned, and scowled. How could so young a child be so crabby? By the time Linda was two, she waddled awkwardly, tilting from right to left with each odd step. Lena hoped the leg braces Ray had made for his two-year-old daughter would help, but she didn't hold much hope. He had cut a broomstick in pieces to fit from her inner knee to ankle, cut and sanded each piece lengthwise, and fastened padded ovals of leather that fit the insides of her calves, held in place by three straps with buckles. The middle strap he tightened gradually over time. She became so accustomed to wearing them from morning till night that she woke her parents by throwing them on their bed in the morning.

Jason with Linda (wearing Ray's braces)

Over time, Lena noted that the legs of her grand daughter were straighter, but Linda still didn't smile much.

Merrilee and Linda, Double First Cousins

Olga's daughter, Merrilee, born that December was an exceptionally beautiful child, and pleasant with dark brown curls. Much more like Lena's own children were years earlier.

1940: Clarence and Vera had been married two years when they were asked to look after Linda when Helen would deliver her third child. Also dropping in that day was the "Waterloo Four" (Donnie was two). Things weren't too bad until three-year-old Merrilee made the mistake of climbing on three-and-a-half year-old, "Crabby Linda's" beloved red tricycle. Merrilee's pretty dress was nearly torn from her back before an uncle--most likely Clarence--peeled the enraged girl off her cousin's back, holding her away from himself to avoid the vicious kicks by the red-faced hellion. The screams were ear-shattering. It was the "Tantrum of All Tantrums." Why he and Vera were still willing to put the little demon in their shiny coupe with a rumble seat and take "it" home with them was a mystery. But they did, and for some unknown reason they both developed a soft spot in their hearts for "Crabby Linda." Their door was always open to her.

1941: World War II began. Franklin Delano Roosevelt had been President since 1933. He served three terms and won the fourth but didn't live to see his peace plan implemented. He was a president much loved by the people he served.

Ray was having difficulty finding employment to sustain his family. When he heard from his sister, Rhoda, that welders were needed in the shipyards of San Leandro, California, and what they were being paid, he packed up his family in his junker of a car and they barely made it over the mountains, and through the desert, to where his sister and brother-in-law lived. Once there, he was hired as a welder for making warships and suddenly life was good. His family lived in a new modern house, he had a good car; and best of all for Helen, he had no drinking buddies. All was good--for a year and a half.

Because of one man's carelessness, a great sheet of steel siding broke two of its three great chains, and it swung, grazing Ray and almost killing him. He had smashed legs, a concussion, a broken arm, and broken ribs. He left the hospital in a wheelchair with metal plates in one leg, and casts on both, as well as an arm. When he was able, and still with one leg in a cast, the family packed up and began the reverse trip back to Minnesota, to live with Lena, Cornelius, and Lloyd.

Ray and Helen established their bedroom in the parlor and music room along with all they owned. Their three children slept upstairs. Karen had the small walk-through bedroom and slept in a green oval trundle bed with a canvas bottom. Jason had the small bedroom straight ahead through Karen's room; and Linda had Henry's old bedroom on the left.

The corner cupboard sat to the right of the doorway. Mothballs could be smelled when its doors were opened. Helen sat on the floor with Linda going through old things. And on seeing a porcelain Betty Boop doll, Linda begged for and got it. That old cupboard held a treasure trove.

Every night, the deep bonging tones of the great grandfather's clock at the base of the stairs would wake Linda up in the night. But in the midst of the moving back in with Lena, Cornelius and Lloyd, pesky Linda complained of not feeling well, so was ignored and sent to bed still complaining. It was not a restful night and the bonging clock made her feel worse. Sleep was a waking nightmare with the corner cupboard stretching, wavering and bending towards her in the moonlight. She tried to turn her eyes to other areas but the room had begun to scare her as it constantly moved, swelled, wavered, until she chose to break the rules and go downstairs where Mom was sleeping. Linda knew not to wake her parents up, as that meant being sent back to her scary room, so she lay down on the bare wood floor by her mother's side of the bed. All the furniture in that room behaved the same as that upstairs—wavering, swelling. But her fear was gone. So that's where her parents found her in the morning and scolded her for not staying in her bed where she belonged. This brought on a storm of hopeless tears, and a very strange sounding voice as she tried to talk. Hoarse and thick. Helen and Lena talked it over and decided to give Linda a pickle to eat to determine if she had mumps since there was swelling on both sides of her throat under the jaw. Not a good plan. Linda hated pickles and squalled simply at having the darn thing in her mouth. Linda did have the mumps. But Lena was the recipient of Helen's worries and care because when Lena's children had mumps in their childhood, Lena, who had never had mumps, didn't get them at that time, and now Helen feared for her mother's health. Linda was quarantined to her room while Helen fretfully watched over Lena.

Lena had grown so accustomed to living in silence that the noise and activity of three young children at times was overwhelming. But to have Helen at her side was wonderful and both women enjoyed their companionship.

Ray had found employment as a mechanic; Jason wandered off by himself, probably into town, seeming to bother no one. While sweet, placid, blonde little Karen loved sitting on Lena's lap. She never fussed and was pleasantly quiet.

The problem was Linda. Even as Lena thought of that one, the door banged and she passed through the room running. This time her path crossed with her mother and Helen could be heard saying in a quiet, but irritated voice, "No running in the house. How many times do you have to be told? And stop slamming the door!"

Lena heard no response from the girl and was sure there was most likely the usual scowl. At least Linda would be out of the house for the weekend again. And she wondered how Vera and Clarence tolerated the unpleasant girl. But they came for her whenever she wasn't in school. And Vera and Clarence made sure she was in church every Sunday, seated between them. Looking quite presentable, too, thanks to Vera.

It troubled Lena knowing she thought of this granddaughter as "the girl" instead of by her name, and she made an effort to be kinder to the "wild child" who seemed to be everywhere and into everything all the time.

The butter churn had caught Linda's attention recently while Lena churned fresh butter as she sat on her bench at the back door. It took a while of watching from a distance, then edging closer, until the girl sat on the end of the bench. Finally, in a small voice she asked, "What are you doing?"

"Churning butter."

Another long pause, "Can I see?"

And Lena removed the top to show Linda the odd-looking cream in the bottom of the wooden churn.

"Can I do it?" came the next question and Lena showed her granddaughter how to move the paddle. She tried, but she wasn't big enough or strong enough so gave the paddle back to Lena. And then she was up, racing away.

Any resolve Lena had to be more attentive to Linda went up in smoke a few days later as Lena came from collecting eggs, and saw the red, enraged face of the furious little girl swinging haymaker fists at her brother's face. He kept pushing her backwards simply by shoving her with the flat of a hand to her forehead, until she screamed at him, "You goddamn sonofabitch!" and aimed a vicious kick towards his nether regions making him leap backwards.

Lena was horrified and went directly to Helen with the full report, finishing with, "Where did she learn to talk like that?"

Lena shared her concerns about the undisciplined girl with Lloyd who agreed she needed a firm hand, which Helen didn't have, and Ray was either blind to or didn't care. Lloyd knew where Linda learned the bad words. Ray was unaware when talking with other men that his daughter was nearby.

Lloyd decided a little discipline needed to be dispensed at the Sunday noon meal when Linda started to leave the table with food still on her plate. Lloyd who had seated himself next to her put a hand out, blocking her exit, saying, "You haven't finished your mashed potatoes."

"I don't want them."

"You took them and you will stay till you eat them."

"I'm not hungry."

"Then you shouldn't have taken them."

"They're cold."

"Then you should have eaten them when they were warm."

"You're not my dad and I don't have to do what you say."

"No, I'm not. But, you do have to do what I say." And there

he sat, while neither parent rescued her; and Jason and Lena watched.

With tears rolling down her face, and everyone else departed, Linda forced the cold congealed mess down her throat, with hate in her heart towards everyone. It was hard being a child in that family.

Lena's avoidance of dentists appeared to have rubbed off on Helen who had all her own upper teeth extracted before she was forty. Oral care for her children was almost non-existent except for an occasional scrub with baking soda on a washrag. Jason and Karen didn't fuss about their teeth, so why did Linda complain about teeth packing with food? Oh! Right! The Pest!! When she began spitting out pieces of tooth, Helen looked in her daughter's mouth and saw three teeth decayed to the gum leaving jagged rims: two lower, one upper, declared them baby teeth and that they would fall out. They weren't baby teeth, but they were falling out—in pieces. (Linda had inherited from some ancestor a lack of enamel coat for those three teeth.) After thinking about the teeth for a short while, Helen decided to have a dentist examine them and early one morning woke Linda, telling her to dress and comb her hair as she would be leaving with her dad to have her teeth looked at by the local dentist in Mabel. Ray drove his daughter down to an empty main street, stopping long enough to point to a worn wood shingle hanging over a door between two stores, saying "That's the doc's name, go on up the stairs, he's on the right—first door. You'll know him by the stogie hangin' out of his mouth." There was no mistaking the large man with the stogie in his mouth.

In no time at all, the shocked girl was seated in a big chair and gripping the arms of it while a stranger pulled her cheeks out to better see her teeth. Years later she had no recall of any injections; only feeling a beefy arm wrap around her head, putting a thumb on her tongue, and holding her jaw down. The second attempt to grip the first lower tooth was successful. With a yank to the left, a yank to the right, then straight up, and the doctor dropped a bloody chunk with a "clink" onto a silver tray right next to his unlit stogie. Back he went, same right-left-up-clink. And once more but with a little variation as it was an upper tooth. Three six-year molars gone by eight years of age. Bloody chunks on the tray with a saliva-soggy stogie, which the dentist put back in his mouth, then turning to send the kid on her way. One look at the lolling head and rolling eyes, his big hand grabbed the back of Linda's neck and shoved her head between her knees. A few minutes later he told her she could go home now--which she had already been instructed by Ray to do. It wasn't a pleasant walk home. On entering the kitchen through the east porch door, a teary Linda watched her mother and grandmother light-heartedly talking and smiling as they busily moved between the large oak table and the cookstove. She watched silently for a minute or two, then walked upstairs to her cot in Henry's old room where she lay down on her back to keep her painful face off the pillow, and began to cry until tears trickled into her ears.

Lena was not particularly fond of Ray's family and had little to visit about with them. His parents came perhaps two times, once with Ray's sister, Rhoda, trailing along. Lena had walked them around the yard after lunch. Making conversation was tiring; listening to the racket of grandkids inside and outside was tiring. Her crooked, painful back was tiring.

Rhoda had grown bored and wandered off by herself. Chickens had gotten out of their pen and wandered freely in the yard. Coming from the big city of Waterloo, Rhoda found it all so boring and dirty. As she passed by her niece, Linda, Rhoda paused and, looking down at the girl, she lifted one of her braids with a finger, then said with a laugh, "Your hair is chicken-shit brown." And wandered on, unaware she had just earned the lifelong dislike of her niece.

Shortly after Lena had seen her guests off and was slowly making her way back towards the house, Lena noticed Linda sitting on her heels playing with something in the grass, holding it close and examining it. But as Linda saw her grandmother approach, she dropped something white, then stood up and went into the house.

Curious, Lena stopped and looked down at the spot Linda had studied but saw only a feather with fresh chicken dropping on it. "Is that crazy girl playing in chicken droppings? What ever in the world is wrong with her?" She was beginning to hope Ray and Helen would soon be able to move into a house of their own.

When Lena became conscious of Linda's expressionless eyes watching her as she visited with Helen, and as she moved about the kitchen fixing meals, it didn't bother her at first, but as time went on and the silent watching continued she wondered what, in heaven's name, was going on in that head?

Lena and Cornelius lived separate lives and had come to stand-offs when issues arose. Lena had finally refused to tolerate her husband's smoking his pipe in the house. When he persisted, she didn't fix his meals. With extra people living in the house Cornelius pushed his limits and brought his pipe out while sitting at the kitchen table, having had coffee.

Lena, with venom dripping, ordered him to "Take that filthy thing outside."

Cornelius was about to refuse when the adversaries noticed Linda quietly watching Lena's face.

Cornelius slowly got up, fingers curled around his pipe, and just as slowly walked out of the kitchen.

Lena, looking back at the silent girl, remembered the last time she'd spoken to her--and wished she could take back the words, "You're nothing but a dirty little liar!"

Those words and tone of voice were echoing in the girl's head, brought back by the venom in Lena's words to the old man seated at the table; and once more she said to herself,

"I'm dirty and I'm little, but I'm not a liar." It would take her over 70 years to forgive her grandmother.

It seemed such a little thing at the time, involving the old couple in the rental house at the bottom of Lena's hill. The old man had come up the path in a hurry one day in an agitated state and spoken to Lena and Helen. After hastily ordering Linda not to leave the yard, Helen had hurried back down with the old man to his house. Something momentous had happened: Lena was distraught and Helen had looked shocked. So Linda had to know what was going on and promptly went to the very edge of the yard—right up to but not beyond it—to get as good a view as possible of what was visible of the neighbors little house. Immediately, Lena was there and snapping at the girl about leaving the yard after being told not to.

Shaking her head, Linda said, "No, I haven't."

And that was when Lena told her granddaughter she was "Nothing but a dirty little liar."

Standing there, in a soiled dress, with bare and dirty feet, uncombed hair, looking up into the furious face of her grandmother Linda knew she was dirty, and little, and that she didn't like her grandmother—but she hadn't lied.

The elderly couple renting the small house on the Erickson farm moved out when the woman, Alma, suffered a debilitating stroke. But to Linda's joy, the people who moved in were Uncle Clarence and Aunt Vera. And, in short order, Linda moved in with them and was given the upstairs bedroom. Vera loved fixing the girl's hair, always pressing the wide taffeta ribbon that formed a bow for her head. A pressed white hanky was always pinned to the front of the dress bodice. Linda may have come home wrinkled, dirty, and messy looking, but she always arrived at school perfectly groomed and happy.

Sunday mornings were especially looked forward to

by Linda, as Vera fixed pancakes, bacon, and eggs, while Clarence sat at the small table and read the Sunday paper before church. Looking up at Vera busy flipping eggs, Linda asked her aunt if her bedroom could have new wallpaper. With the barest of pauses, Vera looked towards Clarence who had the paper open to the colorful "funnies" section, and gently suggested she should ask her uncle. Linda then approached him with her request; and jovially, he put his paper down, pushed his chair away from the table, and scooped the girl onto his lap. Hugging her close he said, "Yes!"

Oh, the joy! And then he added, ever so pleasantly, "We will save up all the pretty "funnies" until we have enough to completely paper your room! How's that!?"

First was the shocked surprise, followed by a clear vision of "funnies" all over the walls. And she laughed and laughed, then rested her head on her uncle's shoulder and visualized comics all over the walls. It was better than wallpaper!

Lena would miss Helen but was relieved when Ray found a small house in Prosper—where Lena's sister-in-law Carrie's home was--where they could afford the rent. It was farther for Ray to his job in Mabel, but easier for Helen to walk to the single grocery store, and to Carrie's house in under five minutes. The family finally moved out of the big house on the hill, and once again Lena had peace and quiet.

Clarence and Vera moved to a small farm just outside of Prosper where Linda often stayed, playing in the barn as her uncle milked their cow while singing "Hard Rock Candy Mountain" and "Rock of Ages" in a strong and pleasant voice. She loved watching the cats sit up, begging, and Clarence squirting milk in their mouths. He was very good at hitting the mark! And Vera sewed dresses for her from feed sacks, and cranked up the Victrola to "play tubes of music." Best of all was to be given a wonderful gray tiger stripe kitten, that Vera helped Linda name. Gramaulkin.

The undisciplined, out-of-control, watcher of people, Linda, reached a conclusion one pleasant day: "Aunt Vera, when I grow up I'm going to marry a man who doesn't drink, who doesn't smoke, and who doesn't swear. I'm going to marry a preacher."

Linda spent as much time as she could with her aunt and uncle, and as far away as she could from her brother. She had started fighting back, tired of being a punching bag, and unaware of how much he followed her. Helen always kept Karen close at her side, while Jason had a way of disappearing; doing what, God only knew. But he always showed up at mealtime and bedtime.

September 2nd, 1945: On her own she explored their new small town, wandering from end-to-end, walking up one side, over the train tracks until she reached the edge of the new highway, then back down the opposite side. She took her time passing the small houses with shady trees lining the street on both sides; she gazed at each house she passed.

On this particular day it was so nice, sunny, warm and peaceful. As she came to a small, square, white house with its windows open to the perfect weather, she was brought to a stop when music floated out from one of the windows. Beautiful, beautiful soaring, perfect music. She had never heard anything like it and didn't know what made it. She listened enthralled till the music died away, then wandered on down the single street towards home. Then suddenly, with no warning, the doors flew open on every house, and windows were thrown up, heads appeared, and people rushed into the street shouting, dancing, hugging, "It's over. It's over —the war is over!" She had a lot to tell her mother when she was home again. There was no radio in their house. When she told of the beautiful music she'd heard, her mother nonchalantly stated, "Oh, that was Hildus, he plays the violin--but only when he's alone.

He's very odd."

Gramaulkin came home with Linda and grew into a big fat cat that followed her like a dog. They were always together; he even followed her to school, yowling all the way. She loved him with all her heart, and the cat seemed to reciprocate, purring loudly, and curling his paws as she carried him upside down, dressed in doll clothes and bonnet. If anyone else tried, there was hissing and spitting. He was hers and hers alone.

And then Gramaulkin disappeared. She searched and cried. And cried and searched, for days during that hot summer. Her mother told her tomcats were like that--he'd come home when he wanted. But he didn't. Eventually, she did find him, a year later as she helped her mother search for Karen who had disappeared. As it turned out the little girl had knocked on the neighbor's door and asked for a cookie. They couldn't resist the angelic looking child and invited her in for the cookie.

In the meantime, Helen sent Linda to search the unused barn behind the neighbor's house while Helen went to the house. The barn wasn't locked; inside it was one big square room completely empty, but boards had been nailed to two upright posts forming a rough ladder to a closed aperture in the ceiling. Struggling up the makeshift ladder to the cover, it was with great difficulty she pushed it up enough to look around another empty room, well-lit by two windows. As she turned her head each way as far as she could, she looked into the mummified face of Gramaulkin, who had died waiting for her. She knew he had been put there. And she knew who did it. Jason! Whatever meant the most to her had a way of breaking—or disappearing.

Linda with Her Gramaulkin

It never occurred to Linda to ask why they moved so often. It had become so routine it had actually become fun exploring all the nooks and crannies of the old houses they would call home. It was only when she was old that she suspected her father drank up the rent money.

Lena's family had grown up and, with the exception of Lloyd, formed their own families, living busy lives and *earning their livings. Cornelius no longer farmed but rented out the land. The barn and pig lot were now empty, and the horses enjoyed their lives in the pasture. Lloyd worked wherever farmers needed his services while still living at home. Even the chicken coop was empty, except for the few running loose, as Lena wasn't up to the work required for them. With no one to clip their wings, they flew over the fences and took to roosting in the apple trees. The cats must have died from some feline disorder: Linda found the last one curled up in the hollow of one of the trees in the orchard.*

Lena's two daughters were frequently in touch, being married to two brothers; and the five cousins were exceptionally close being "double first-cousins."

Summer was always a good time for the two families to get together--the City Slickers and the Country Bumpkins, as coined by Linda and Merrilee. The 4th of July was a favorite holiday to spend with Lena and Cornelius on the farm; though "the watcher" noticed no tears were ever shed on their departure. Especially after Merrilee and Linda had a pillow fight in Henry's old bedroom and knocked the entire storm window out and to the ground. Being summer, the inner window had been fully raised, and the lift-up wood that covered a vent at the bottom of the "storm" was open in an effort to cool the room. A direct hit with the pillow sent the storm window, unbroken, to the thick grass. "The watcher" also noted Lloyd was angry.

Jake had picked up quite a good supply of fireworks in Waterloo that he wanted to share with family outside of any town or authorities, so he packed up his family and their chocolate-colored dog, Skimpy, in his new car, and headed for his in-laws farm. There were some in the family who believed Lloyd thought of his "in-laws" as "out-laws."

The weather was perfect, sunny and warm. The cousins ran freely everywhere. Skimpy rolled in chicken poop and had to be washed, while the two brothers with Lloyd spent the day improvising a launch pad for the rockets. Lloyd found old eavestroughs that they fastened into one long one and cobbled together a shaky launch pad in the pasture beside the house. It was hard waiting for the sun to set and the darkness to come. But at last the great moment arrived, with Skimpy safely shut up in the fine new car. And Merrilee had thoughtfully rolled one window open a small way for coolness. The grandparents were given ringside seats on the kitchen porch to watch from a distance while everyone else crawled through the fence. The children were minus their shoes because if poop was stepped in, it was easier washing feet than cleaning shoes.

Then the men placed, and lit, the first rocket and stepped back. All eyes watched as it started up the long trough. Then everyone gasped as the launch pad slowly tilted towards the house and would, in a fraction of time, be aimed at two old people on their porch. A mad dash took place by all three men and it was shoved back. The first spectacular explosion burst forth in glorious sparkles and lights, and colors. Oh! It was all too wonderful!! Having fixed the launching problem, the rest of the rockets and whirligigs lit up the hilltop over Mabel with great explosions. It was the best 4th of July ever!

It was the aftermath that wasn't so good. When Merrilee and Linda let Skimpy, the "stinkende-hunden" out of Jake's new car, his dark fur was dotted with chunks of white cotton from the torn-up seat cushions. Even the roof covering was torn. Worse, the dog bit the open edge of the window breaking it in many pieces. "Chewed up" would be most accurate.

Uncle Jake was not happy. And neither was Uncle Lloyd the next day when he had to retrieve his horses, which had jumped their fences and were found grazing in fields belonging to other people, almost two miles away.

The "watcher" hoped every 4th of July would be as much fun, but no one ever suggested fireworks again. And as the city folk prepared to leave the next day, Skimpy rolled in

*poop one more time. They all left unsmiling in a tattered car
with all the windows down.*

Lena's back made any movement painful for her. Doctors
had no fix to offer her and slowly, inexorably she walked bent
forward, tilted to one side, one shoulder blade giving a hump-
like look beneath her clothes. She never complained, though
she did see several different doctors. One doctor had recom-
mended a skilled seamstress in Cresco whose reputation in
fitting people with a comfortable supportive vest might give
Lena some relief. With Helen, and Linda, accompanying her,
Lloyd drove them to Grace Nash's shop in Cresco to have Lena
fitted with elasticized support, while for modesty's sake, Linda
was sent to cool her heels sitting on the outside steps.

There seemed to be some relief from the garment, but year-
by-year Lena eventually became no taller than Cornelius. The
hard work, joyless life, and deprivation took its toll and Lena
looked older than her years with paper-like dry skin, faded,
tired eyes behind glasses, hair that was thin, grayish yellow,
and always pulled back in a tight bun. It was hard to see anything of the beautiful girl she had been, but glimpses were seen
by Linda in the interactions of Lena with her daughters when
Lena's face would be lit with a smile, and from somewhere
deep inside her something beautiful glowed in her eyes and
across her face; a peaceful softening for a few seconds. She
tended towards silence, and essentially never left the ghostly
gray house she had no love for. She avoided the presence of
the man she was shackled to--who now showed open disgust
when he looked at her. He did his pipe smoking outside in
nice weather; and when it was too cold or inclement, smoked
in the privacy of his bedroom.

Lena had long ago lost interest in dressing up, and wore
plain, shapeless cotton dresses in which she tried to hide her
crooked bony form. Jewelry she never owned. She looked
stern and thin-lipped. She no longer attended church as the

pain of sitting motionless in hard pews added to her pains. It seemed as though the life had been sucked from her leaving only a shell.

Cornelius aged better, keeping a straight back, ruddy color and thick head of hair that kept its reddish tones with a sprinkling of gray into his late seventies. A few pictures exist of Lena holding several different grandbabies at different times. There are none of Cornelius with any grandchildren at any time.

One grand daughter spoke to him only once in her life, even having lived in the same house with him for extended periods of time, later admitting to not liking him, and being afraid of him. As Cornelius sat on the bench at the back door, with his sweater vest buttoned to the neck, wearing baggy-kneed wool trousers and dark jacket, he placed the walking stick he always carried, against the house, and reached inside the vest to pull out a small paper bag of white peppermints. As he opened it with stiff, gnarled fingers, he felt her presence. He hadn't heard her but standing out of reach of his cane was "the scrapper"--the one that drove Lena crazy. He looked closer at her. Holding the open sack in her direction, he said, "Do you want a candy?"

She still kept her distance but shrugged a shoulder and answered a quiet, "I don't care." Whereupon, he reached into the sack, and taking out one candy, he put it in his mouth, closed up the bag and put it back inside his vest. He then turned his gaze and thoughts back to the empty pig pen.

Surprise flickered across her face, then something shut down towards the old man, and she backed away. It was the only time she ever spoke to her grandfather.

Ray moved his family from Prosper into the center of Hesper--as small a town as the one they'd just left, but now only three miles to work for Ray. This house was musty and mildewed, but as usual, Helen never did complain or showed worry about anything. She simply went about the business of feeding her family, doing the laundry in the back yard with an old gas-powered washer. Sewing girls' dresses on an old treadle Singer, the patterns made by having her daughters lie down on newspapers and tracing around them for size, then cut her own designs. She always had a garden and canned the vegetables. And she hummed. While she worked, she always hummed. She was her mother's daughter.

It remains a mystery how she and Ray moved the big piano from the house on the hill into the latest home. But there it was. And Linda got piano lessons from--wait for it...old John Bates at 25-cents a half-hour!

Then in a matter of months the slumlord wanted to live in the house himself and had the Kepharts move again--to a quite nice farmhouse one-and-a-half miles west of Hesper. The stay there was to be short but memorable when Karen contracted bulbar polio and was taken to Mayo in Rochester, Minnesota where miraculously she came out of her coma under the selfless care of the Catholic nuns. Jason and Linda were quarantined in their home but still experienced shunning when allowed back in school. And of course, the family moved again when their new landlord accused Ray of not paying his rent, while Ray insisted he had paid (but knew the homeowner wasn't sober at the time). Who was telling the truth will never be known.

While Lena knew all was not right for Helen, she didn't begin to know the poverty of her daughter's life, or how trapped she was. And the next house was one more move downwards into a deteriorated old house at the end of a very long dirt and grass lane, deep in woodland. No electricity, of course. No running water. And no functional garden area. School was a long walk by the dirt and gravel roads, so Helen's children explored the woods finding a shorter, more pleasant way to school by climbing fences and cutting through farmers' properties. It was still a long walk, and in the winter the darkness would be coming on by the time they were home.

It was cold. The snow was deep, and they were tired. No sooner were the boots off and coats hung up when Helen anxiously approached Linda. Holding a quarter out, she asked her to go back into Hesper to buy a loaf of bread to make sandwiches for Dad's lunch the next day. Not wanting to go back out in the fading light, and being tired, Linda responded, "Ask Jason." Desperation was creeping into Helen's voice as she answered, "He refused. Please. You can keep the change." It wasn't keeping the change that caused the girl to bundle back up and reluctantly start the long walk again. It was her mother having to part with a nickel change that showed how much that loaf of bread was needed. So she went, hurrying, trying to make the best use of the light while she could. Down the lane, past the corncrib, along the fence line to the fallen tree they all climbed over into the woods. Then following the creek past "half-way-home-spring," through more forest, to a pasture, another fence line, and at last—road. Then passing the school, it was two blocks to the only store in town. Shadowy, darkening now—and the store door was locked. Inside the owner's wife, Verna, was busy cleaning the cold meat case near the back of the store. Linda had to knock loudly, grateful that the kind woman let her in and sold her the 20-cent loaf of Sunbeam bread, gave her a nickel change—then locked the door after her. With feelings of dread now, and nearly racing to be home, Linda began the reverse trip. Reaching the woods she was now guided by the giant winter moon, which is a beautiful thing, and was comforting. Everything was so lit up by it. But it also gave the trees a skeletal look of black, claw-like hands and arms that made matching shadows of themselves on the snow below. It seemed an endless trek past the spring and on to the barbed-wire by the fallen tree which was harder getting over from this side of it, but at last, with relief, she was out of the woods and passing cleared cornfields. In the distance, the corn crib could be seen, Linda thought the trip was about to end until she saw two black lines wavering on the moonlit snow, passing the corncrib. Stopping, she studied the two odd lines—and then her nose told her "skunk!" No! She did not need this! Walking slowly, timing the skunk's slow waddle till it passed a safe distance from the corncrib, she moved close to its weathered side while keeping one eye on the skunk. The faint light of the kerosene lamp could be seen. Home! She'd made it. Then out of the dark side of the corncrib something leaped at her, roaring, long arms extended! Linda fell face down in the snow, screaming in hysterics, throwing the bread. And heard her brother laughing joyfully as he ran away. Pulling herself together, snow and tears on her face, found the bread and went to her mother, telling her what Jason had done. "Well, you're here now," said her mother, smiling--and went back to her tasks, humming.

That same winter, approximately two months later, Karen and Linda made their way home from a day at school in the tiny town of Hesper without Jason—didn't know where he was, nor did they care. As they began the wintry walk a weak sun softened the cold, giving enough warmth to have done slight surface melting. Leaving the road and going through the pasture land after climbing a fence, the sisters walked up and down the low hills, through valleys and into the thick woods to the "half-way-home-spring". There Karen stopped and knelt on a flat rock. That annoyed Linda, who told her to keep moving. But she refused. She wanted a drink. She insisted it was a "spring" and therefore safe to drink—and drink she was going to. But not Linda! She waited, standing by a giant old tree--very big around with bare sides (this should have been a clue) and looked around at all the bareness--not a bush or scrub, just frozen mud all around the area. (This should have been a second clue). Then her *wandering eyes moved across the creek, up the tree-covered hill, but bare ground, and stared directly into the horrible eyes of a wild boar! Its reaction was instant--it came down that hill, across the creek, mouth wide open, directly at Linda! That monster chased her three times around the tree, snapping at her heels, its cloven hooves slipping in the mud slime over the frozen ground! Glaring yellow eyes, raised bristles all down the spine, upper and lower fangs, mere inches behind her. Screaming on every rotation, Linda ran, looking back several times in terror. On the third round the monster looked straight ahead at the still-kneeling, but gaping Karen, unable to move—and it went like a speeding train straight at her! Over and over Linda screamed for her sister to "Run! Run! Run!" But there she knelt, staring at what was coming till in the last moment she grasped an object in the mud, pulling, tugging, trying to break it loose from the ground. Then realizing she couldn't, she let go and threw herself sideways just as the beast reached her. Whatever she'd been struggling with snapped back towards its place in the mud, but first struck a sharp snap to the boar's snout, stopping it in its tracks. It raced back across the creek and up the hill. Linda's belief in guardian angels became unshakeable.*

Lena woke to a cold house but didn't think on it much. It was the last day of January after all. Dressing quickly as possible in multiple layers of clothing, she made her painful way to the kitchen, but paused by the coal stove. It should have been putting out more heat by now. Maybe Cornelius got a late start that morning. But in the kitchen range no fire burned at all. Was she being punished again for the acrimonious exchange that had occurred yesterday? Angry words that had been said many times, in many ways, over the years--so why this childishness now? Fine. She would get the stove going. It's not as if she didn't know how. And she set about with paper, fine dry kindling, and matches, and soon could feel the welcome heat.

Unable to lift anything of much weight, Lena had a small cart on wheels which she pushed from pantry to stove when she transported water for dish washing, or bringing the large coffee pot to percolate on the range. She wheeled the heavy container as close as she could, then awkwardly got it to the edge of the stovetop and pushed it into place. She didn't want to play the childish "punishment game" with Cornelius but things only got worse when he felt he'd "won." He would be fixing his own breakfast again; and if he left a mess he'd fix his own lunch as well. Getting a small pan and filling it with water, she boiled an egg for herself, and then cutting a thick slice of bread, she toasted it on a long meat fork holding it over the open flame.

It was hard reading her Bible now; she needed new glasses but wondered if it was worth the effort and money to see an eye doctor. She needed this time in the morning with the words that comforted and kept her going.

The sun was bright this morning in spite of the cold. Lloyd was staying nights at the farm he was choring for while the farmer recovered from the broken leg one of his milk cows had given him. She missed Lloyd's company most, but also all his help with wood and water. Her children had all grown into such fine, good people, and she was proud of them. And all remained good church goers as well as their spouses--with the exception of Ray. She had much to be grateful for. Helen she worried about. She had always seemed to be in a world of her making; dreamy, happy seeming. But Lena knew Helen lived a life of hardship, making do with so little, working hard; and acting like all was well in her world. Something wasn't right.

Lena had a crank telephone now. A big oak box on her kitchen wall. And even though REA had begun bringing electricity to rural areas since 1930, lamps still lit the Erickson home. The telephone had been the only modernization in the house in 49 years. Now Helen was the only one with kerosene lamps and no telephone. Olga occasionally called from

Waterloo, and Clarence also checked in by telephone. And they all had cars. Odd that Cornelius never wanted one; he was a stubborn man!

The days seemed so long and empty to her. All her favorite relatives and friends had died or moved away. The days of quilting and sewing were long in the past. It was impossible now to clean out areas, and what few cupboards there were required a ladder to reach the top shelves. She still had her small "woman's" ladder, but the days of climbing it were also over. She tried to keep up with the laundry by hand washing a few things every day, drying them on a clothes rack in the living room.

When the grandfather clock chimed 9 am, Lena felt an uneasiness that Cornelius hadn't put in an appearance. Walking through the living room to where the clock stood at the base of the stairs, she listened for sounds of movement, and heard nothing. She hadn't climbed those stairs in years. She had told him he could clean his own room and bring his own laundry down, many years ago when she banned him from her bedroom.

Lloyd had set up his own bed in the music room, so she had no reason to go upstairs. And now she dreaded making the trip. Calling his name as loudly as she could, and still hearing nothing, she had no other choice than to climb the long flight of steps. At the top, turning to her right and looking down the long dark hall, she raised her voice again. And again, no response. Something told her not all was well with Cornelius. Placing one foot in front of the other, it was with dread she entered the room at the end of the hall. Sun flowed in through the un-curtained windows. Looking to her right at the bed against the end wall of the narrow room, Lena could see the mound that was Cornelius' body beneath the heavy winter blankets. There was staleness, and tobacco odor in the air. And silence. Feeling shaky, she came close to the bedside and leaned close, trying to see clearly. He didn't move, though she spoke his name, and reached out a cold shaky hand to touch his face. He was warm. She shook his shoulder eliciting no response, then moved the blankets down from his chest and put a hand on him and felt a slight rise and fall of breathing. Turning to his dresser, she picked up his hand mirror and held it under his nose. A slight fogging appeared. Covering him again, she left with as much speed as she could muster, back down the steps to the telephone where she asked the operator to send a doctor. Help was quick to arrive and Lena directed the doctor to the stairs with directions to the bedroom but did not attempt to follow. Within minutes the doctor was back down to the kitchen calling an ambulance.

Cornelius was carried out on a stretcher and taken to the small Rushford hospital. He had had a severe stroke. After several days he was returned to his home where a bed replaced the library table in the living room and he could be near the stove. He was unable to form words, though he tried, and was unable to help himself in any way. His sons helped with the more personal care. The family helped Lena with trying to give Cornelius the liquids and sustenance prescribed by the doctor, but the prognosis was not good. Clarence and Lloyd asked Lena for all pertinent papers concerning the farm, a will, his finances after having searched his room and finding nothing. But Cornelius had excluded Lena from everything and she could tell them nothing, other than years ago he had an old wood box he kept things in. The men then searched the entire upstairs and still found nothing. They had to rely on the bank for any information about the farm and finances. The missing sailor's desk became such a troubling thing to Lena she could think of nothing else.

Lloyd had to return to his farm job for a few more days but checked in often by phone. Help came and went, and Lena did what she could to keep her restless husband comfortable. Time dragged. Unable to stand doing nothing on a long afternoon, her thoughts returned to the missing desk!

1949

A TIME TO KEEP SILENCE
AND A TIME TO SPEAK

Lena found herself once more upstairs, wandering the rooms and wondering what Cornelius had done with the precious desk. Returning to the smelly, dreary room she started with the walls, feeling and tapping all around the room. No secret hide-away. She looked then at the floor and taking up the walking stick began tapping back and forth across the old wood floor. From side to side of the room she worked toward where the bed was, hoping what she looked for wasn't under the floor beneath the bed. When she reached the large rag-rug beside the bed she laid the stick on the blanket and with a little effort dragged the rug out of the way and resumed the tapping.

The change in sound was sudden, stopping her in her tracks. Looking more closely and tapping again, she knew something solid was beneath an area the size of the sailor's box. She could see, now that she knew, what had been done. There were well-disguised lines of wood fitted to form the cover of the hidden place in the floor. But next was the quandary of how to raise the cover from its place. The only mark notice-able in the area of wood looked like a large nail hole. With her mind racing, Lena knew she'd never be able to pry up the wood with a nail, but a knob with a screw was a different thing altogether. She couldn't remember when she'd felt such excitement. Turning to the different pieces of furniture, she looked for a knob attached with a screw. There! There on the washstand--the drawer had two of what she wanted. One was tight, one was loose. She removed the loose one, and slowly with effort screwed the knob into the nail hole. Knowing her physical limitations, she dropped a pillow where she needed to kneel, then assessed the nearness of the bed she would need to lever herself back up. It seemed close enough, but to be sure, she dragged a chair even closer, and then very care-fully lowered herself till she knelt on the pillow. Then grasping the knob, she pulled straight up. It had been snugly fit, but the cover lifted and she was looking down at the faded blue-red lid of the old box Cornelius had kept locked and hidden from her all these years. It was hard lifting the heavy thing from the hole in the floor, but no amount of pain would stop her now. With the box resting on the bed, she turned her atten-tion to getting herself up from the floor by resting her arms on the bed, turning her knees in the same direction, and pushing herself up leaning over the bed. It was slow, hard, and painful. She sat by the box, resting, for a few minutes, then reaching into an apron pocket, withdrew the watch fob with its keys--the keys Cornelius had always kept so close. Looking at each of the keys she chose the one that looked the oldest, and it slipped into the key opening easily--and clicked. Lena raised the lid not knowing what to expect.

Papers that looked old lay on top of old newspapers. Spreading the papers out on her lap, then picking up first one, then another, bringing each in turn up close to read. She knew she had found the deed to the property. But no will. Laying those aside she picked up an old newspaper dated June 1898. Puzzled, she picked up the one from beneath the first--also from June 1898. One more rested in the box and that one was March 1897. That one she slowly began to scan wondering why the papers had been saved, but also why they were hidden; locked away, and then she knew: the main story on the front page was of her brother Hendriek's accidental death. Hurriedly, she picked up a second paper--1898 June, scanning until on the third page a short piece on an empty house burning down which had belonged to Lars Henderson. Arson was suspected. Picking up the third paper, she discovered it was all about the disappearance of a local man. She felt frozen, shocked,--and unable to stop the search through Cornelius' hoard of secrets. What had he done? The old address book of his family was still there, and his citizenship papers. But only one tin of his smelly tobacco lay on the bottom of the chest.

As she reached for it, she glanced towards his dresser top at the tins of tobacco next to two of his pipes. Then, picking up the tin she gave it a toss to the bed, and heard a rattle as it landed. Picking it back up, she shook it and heard again a metallic rattle. Prying and twisting the lid, she worked the cover off. When she saw what lay inside, she knew from the blackness closing in on her vision she was about to faint. She could only tilt to one side in an effort to lie down; she needed to restore blood to her head. Keeping her grip on the open tin as she regained some sense of normalcy. Still not sitting upright for some time, she tipped what was in the tin into her hand and recognized the emerald ring Lars had given her. His grandmother's birthstone ring. Reset.

The afternoon was nearly gone and Lena still sat on the stale bed in the musty room. Her thoughts were all so terrible, and her emotions raced from one end of the spectrum to the other. The house was cooling, the stoves needed tending. HE needed tending. But she knew she would never again be able to even be in the same room with him without wanting to kill him.

That was where Lloyd found her when he came home from his work. The lamps needed to be lit; why had the stoves burned down? As he raced through the rooms, he touched his father--warm and breathing; on into Lena's room where nothing was disturbed. Shouting "Ma" as he went, he finally heard a faint answer from the upstairs. He followed her voice in the dimness, to where she sat on the bed's edge, holding up one hand and calling to him to stop. Turning to a lamp on the dresser he lit it and carried it towards his mother with disorder surrounding her, and a hole in the floor. Setting the lamp on the washstand, he took off his coat and covered Lena's shoulders before sitting down beside her.

And finally Lena poured out the story of the box's history and the meaning of its contents. Lloyd listened in silence; he had no illusions about his father and had tried to provide a protective shield to Lena for years. Just as Lena had tried to fill the void of a bad father for her son, he had tried to make up the void left by a bad husband. Lloyd would keep her secrets. Now he told her he would help her to her room, then get the stoves going, and call for Clarence and Vera to look after Pa.

Following his call to Clarence, he went back upstairs and took the contents of the box down to the stove, except for the legal papers, and burned them. Then he broke the lock on the box and threw the key down the outhouse.

Vera set about fixing a late meal for the two men, but Lena didn't feel well enough to eat and had gotten into her bed. January 31st had been a terrible day.

On February 2, 1949 Cornelius died aged 86 years. As the family gathered around the coffin to pay their last respects, faces showed little emotion. When Lena heard a sniffle from Olga, she turned to her daughter saying, "Don't waste your tears on him. He wasn't worth it."

Lena chose to stay in the gray empty old house, with Lloyd there to fill the wood and coal stock; making sure the water containers were filled with fresh water. And he carried out all used water. He came home each night from wherever he worked for local farmers who all depended on him. And every Saturday night at the town bar, he enjoyed his two beers.

Every Sunday morning he rang the bells of church, summoning the faithful. And he never missed church, though Lena no longer went. She managed the simple meals for the two of them, and the small daily hand laundry. Empty day followed empty day. But painful memories swirled like a tempest in Lena's mind, changing into nightmares in her sleep. She believed if not for her, Lars and Hendriek would not have died. If Cornelius had never knocked on their door how different everyone's life would be.

1950

A TIME TO LOVE AND A TIME TO HATE

Lena struggled in her faith for a long time, trying to overcome the outright hate she felt for Cornelius, but everything circled back to all the loss, the pain, and destruction Cornelius had brought on everyone Lena had loved. When she remembered the two whose lives were gone so early, she raged at God for His permitting it. Now she could see the awfulness of the man she'd married and inwardly she raged at herself to have been so blind, so weak. Her own children had lived with and seen the meanness and brutality. They had been rejected by the very one who should have been the greatest protector in their young lives. Something critical had been missing in the man, but why?—WHY?—had she been ensnared in his web? Her own father had been fooled into believing Cornelius loved his daughter and would make a good life for her. Now in retrospect, Lena wondered if her farr had eventually seen through the mask her husband wore. Was that why his visits stopped and he closed himself off from everyone after his Karen died? And Karen had literally willed herself out of this world when Olga died, as though she could tolerate no more.

Lena had figured out finally that Cornelius had never loved her when she remembered his distaste and disgust of her in times of sickness and pregnancy, and then as she aged. He had felt only lust for her at the beginning. Thinking of her life spent in his terrible presence could at times make her feel physically ill. For three years Lena raged and grieved as Lloyd quietly watched.

The time had come when he felt Helen needed to know Ma wasn't doing well. She was even thinner, and more haggard. He could hear her up in the night, sleepless, walking about. He felt it was time to share some of the devastating facts that had come out those days before Pa died.

He drove his Model T relic the eight miles west to see her. She and Ray now rented a house outside prosper owned by a farmer who had acquired the house when he bought the land. It was the best the family had lived in for years: no plumbing, but it did have electricity and a crank telephone.

And Lloyd was fully aware of Ray's drinking. Jason had dropped out of school after 8th grade and was running wild; but Karen and Linda were bused to school in Canton.

After the talk with Helen, Lloyd drove the mile and a half to the "one cow-six chickens-two cats" gentleman's acreage of Clarence and Vera to discuss the plan for Lena.

And the decision was made that she would be most comfortable with her daughter in spite of the over-crowded house.

Linda was moved out of the small ground-floor bedroom off the living room and installed briefly on the enclosed front porch. Helen and Ray had the big room upstairs; Jason had the small room across the hall from them.

Karen, bless her soul, slept in the walk-in attic. Ah, yes. The walk-in attic where Karen accidentally gave her sister whiplash and concussion with a walloping backward kick right between the eyes as a reward for hiding under Karen's bed and then touching her ankle when she sat down. Christmas vacation for Linda was spent flat on her back on a cot in the kitchen with occasional sips of water and a burning fever. And once again, she knew for a fact that what some relative had once said about getting sick in this family was true. "You have two choices. You can get well, or you can die, but you ain't goin' to the doctor." The choice had to be to get well, school was starting, so she rose from her cot, hair matted to a rat's nest at the nape of her neck, cleaned up as best she could and went to school where her best friend said, "You look thin."

When quiet, disciplined Lloyd brought Lena to live under Ray's roof, he brought calmness to Helen who seemed close to breaking. Lloyd was present on weekends at the Kephart home and took over the sunporch makeshift bedroom since Linda moved into Jason's vacated room when he went into the army. Lloyd quietly watched over his mother and sister but never put his feet under Ray's table or ate a meal with him. Years would pass before Linda realized Lloyd had helped with food and rent money. And Helen lived in that house for four years with her mother, the longest stay after so many moves.

It was hard for Lena's children to tell her it would be better for her staying with Helen. And harder still for Lena to give up her independence, but she listened to Lloyd's patient reasoning and knew he was right. The times of no choices, no options comes to everyone if they live long enough, so the day came when Lena's brass bed was set up in the small bedroom downstairs and the washstand placed in a corner near the head of the bed. A commode sat in the opposite corner. And Lena was moved in.

Helen was pretty much the same with her mother as she was with her children. There, and not there. Physical needs were always met; and Helen placidly went about her work, humming.

Lena napped. Lena thought long thoughts sitting in the platform rocker by the heater. Helen used her spare time stitching a quilt on its frame in a corner of the living room, next to the piano which she still played. And the two women talked over many things. Things that needed to be said in spite of the pain. The time had come to leave the bad, the hateful behind.

Gradually Lena let go of the guilt she had been hanging onto so fiercely. The nightmares stopped. And the painfulness of such a simple thing as rising from the rocker brought home to her that she could no longer care for herself.

Linda had heard the pain-wracked whispered "My, my, my's" of Lena as she got up to move to the supper table. She was never made to feel unwelcome and she was grateful for that. When Lena had admired the rosebud wallpaper in her small room, Helen had said, "Yes, Linda wanted flowers on her walls." Lena didn't see her grandchildren much since the girls left early for school, and since Jason's lack of self-discipline had finally gotten him in trouble with the law. The local sheriff in Mabel had a little talk with him about his options. "Son, you can go into the army, or you can go to jail. Your choice." Jason chose the army.

For the last two summers before she graduated, Linda left to work at a Bible camp on Lake Frontenac, earning the money to buy her school clothes. Amazing how the wild one had gotten herself under control.

During the winter the family had their night out and grocery-buying on Saturday night and Lena had assured Helen she would be fine until they returned, but it was Linda who kept her company, saying she was saving her allowance for a dress she wanted from the Monkey Ward Catalogue.

It was those nights Lena and Linda began to finally converse with each other. Not a lot at first, but the stiffness gradually softened.

The last time they had together was just before Linda packed her bags and prepared to leave home. Linda had helped Lena into bed, tried to make her as comfortable as possible, then asked, "Would you like me to read something to you, Gramma?"

"Why, yes, I would. I'd love to hear the 23rd Psalm." When the Psalm-reading was finished, Lena thanked her grand-daughter for being so kind. The girl didn't answer but reached out a hand and gently touched her grandmother's shoulder.

1956

A TIME FOR WAR AND
A TIME FOR PEACE

Lena

I *wasn't present when my grandmother died. What I know of those hours comes from Lena's two daughters. Hearing of how she sang her "Farewell Lullabies" touched me deeply, and I believe my grandmother was singing her way to Heaven, joyful to be free at last.*

My uncles, being typical men, kept their feelings and memories to themselves. I wish they hadn't. Gramma raised four wonderful people I've loved and cherished in my life, who had such influence on the person I am. I love my Lord. I love my church. And I did grow up to marry a man who didn't drink, didn't smoke, and didn't swear. And he was a preacher.

My Uncle Clarence sang and talked to me, and something he said keeps coming back to me: "There's a little bit of bad in the best of us. And a little bit of good in the worst of us. So it does not behoove the best of us to point the finger at the rest of us."

I am convinced there are no unflawed people--just flawed individuals doing the best they can, with what they have, in whatever place they somehow arrived at. This was my family. I have tried to write with kindness. It is not my job to judge anyone.

For over fifty years I have felt as though I had a household in my head, with people I didn't really know, opening doors, coming and going, beckoning. One I knew was my grandmother. Now I have put on paper the skeleton of truth and wrapped it in the flesh of fiction. This is just a story of my memories, and my imagination.

Minnesota's Norwegian Statehood Pioneer Project

Honors

Cornelius Erickson

who settled in

Newburg Township, Fillmore County

during or before

1900

and Direct Descendant

Linda Mae (Kephart) Nash

Anne Sladky
NSPP Coordinator

Issued May 8, 2020

Minnesota's Norwegian Statehood Pioneer Project

Honors

Hans and Borgina Erickson

who settled in

Newburg Township, Fillmore County

during or before

1905

and Direct Descendant

Linda Mae (Kephart) Nash

Anne Sladky
NSPP Coordinator

Issued May 8, 2020

Book by Linda Nash Will Be A *SMASH* Hit
by
Curt Swarm, Writer, Metal Sculptor, Photographer, Creative
Writing Teacher and Author of the
"Empty Nest" Newspaper Column

Quite literally, I believe "When the Tempest Passes," by 83 year old Linda Nash, is THE Great American Novel of the 21st Century! And I don't give out praise of this nature willy-nilly. Let's see, in the 19th Century we have Melville's "Moby Dick." The 20th Century saw F. Scott Fitzgerald's, "The Great Gatsby." Now we have Linda Nash for the 21st.

Linda attended my creative writing class, and I had the distinct pleasure and honor of editing and proofing this, her first book. I went through it word for word three times, and each time it brought tears to my eyes (I don't cry easily) and impressed me even more with each reading as to her writing ability and story-telling expertise. She uses very effectively some uncanny writing techniques that only the most skilled writers dare employ.

You don't "teach" creative writing. You just give the students the platform and opportunity to write, then get out of their way. Linda's talent is raw, pure, and unlike any I have ever read (and I've read quite a few). I would compare her writing to Willa Cather, W. Somerset Maugham, Emily Dickinson, Charles Frazier, Harriet Beecher Stowe, and Harper Lee—only Linda Nash's writing is superior to these famous authors. No bull.Don't miss the chance to get her first edition, self-published book and make sure you have her sign it.

CPSIA information can be obtained
at www.ICGtesting.com
Printed in the USA
LVHW021134301220
675311LV00006B/35